WHIT

Jack Norman

SILVER MOON BOOKS LIMITED
PO Box CR25, Leeds LS7 3TN

SILVER MOON BOOKS INCORPORATED
PO Box 1614 New York NY 100156

Printed and bound in Great Britain

New authors welcome

Silver Moon Books of Leeds and Silver Moon Books of London are in no way connected.

If you like one of our books you will probably like them all!

For free 20 page booklet of extracts from our first 16 books (and, if you wish to be on our confidential mailing list, from new monthly titles as they are published) please write to:-

Silver Moon Reader Services, PO Box CR 25
Leeds LS7 3TN
or
Silver Moon Books Incorporated
PO Box 1614 New York NY 100156

Surely the most erotic freebie ever!!

CHAPTER ONE

Two women knelt, naked, hands clasped behind their necks. Their backs were ramrod straight, breasts thrust forward, stomachs taut, and knees spaced widely apart. A nude man, dark and handsome, knelt beside them, his heavy sex erect and glistening.

"Part of their daily routine," explained one of the two men watching through the glass.

"Look, I'm not -"

"That one, for example," the Host continued. "Twenty-five years old and married to a stockbroker - a millionaire, like yourself. Once she displayed absolute outrage at any affront to her modesty. Observe."

A man clad in a strange livery of red jacket, black breeches, white stockings and patent leather shoes entered. They could not hear his order through the glass but, without demur, the woman rose to her feet and turned in one graceful movement. She hurried to kneel before the costumed man and began to unbutton his breeches. Taking his large, limp member, she caressed it expertly with her lips, quickly encouraging an erection. The other woman and the naked man remained immobile.

"This viewing room enables potential buyers to discreetly appraise our stock."

"I am not a potential buyer," the visitor insisted, nevertheless assessing the exquisite young woman who knelt before the glass. The hair was shaven from her body and she proudly displayed firm, perfectly formed breasts, badged with honey-coloured aureolae and thrusting nipples. Her midriff was pleasingly taut and, below, the denuded lips of her cleft were enticingly parted.

"Perhaps you would be more interested in the male?"

"No."

"Our prices are reasonable, considering that we have invested a lot of time and money in each of them. Perhaps you would care to make an offer?"

"I do not buy women - or men."

The visitor made little effort to conceal his contempt. Wealthy and handsome, he experienced little difficulty in obtaining the company of desirable women. Presently, the door in the training room opened once more and another naked woman entered. The visitor gasped.

"Unlike the other specimens, this one is not for open sale," the Host said, pausing before adding meaningfully, "yet."

"I don't understand -"

"Your wife, I believe?"

"It can't be!"

Beyond the glass, the valet looked up from his pleasure and spoke. The newcomer moved to stand prettily in front of the glass, only inches away from the visitor, her husband, who scrutinised the delightful creature in disbelief. Always attractive, she was now incredibly beautiful. It was definitely his wife, alive, but the organisation had transformed her.

"Her breasts were rather inadequate: we have had them shaped and augmented. And her nose was less than perfect but we have corrected that. She was a little overweight, of course. We could probably achieve such results with any woman - anyone's wife."

"I will destroy you," the visitor hissed with venom, and two large men who had been standing quietly at the rear of the viewing room now moved quietly forward. The visitor prudently controlled his rage.

"We have not achieved such perfection without pain, effort and expense," the Host continued. "See how vital and alive she is now? Your wife has become accomplished in the erotic arts. She greatly entertained one of our more demanding guests only last night."

In obedient and unquestioning response to a command, the woman slowly and deliberately began to caress her shaven slit.

"She has embraced her slavery as you can see. We freed her mind and released her from society's inhibitions. She, like all of our other acquisitions, can enjoy the punishments and discipline, because she is safe in the knowledge that we would never damage her. My rules do not allow maiming, breaking of the skin or burning, for example."

The guest was barely containing his rage. "You are insane!"

"Shall we say half a million?"

"Quite mad!"

"We can simply sell her to someone else. Regrettably, not for half a million pounds, but I assure you that we would turn a profit."

The man watched, agonised, as his young wife lasciviously stroked her feminine intimacies. Was she aware that people watched? Probably. She undoubtedly knew of the two-way mirror. The delectable creature caressed her magnificent firm breasts, teasing the pert nipples into protruding hardness. Her tongue flicked out salaciously as she gazed at her own reflection.

"The other one has proved a problem," the Host said casually, indicating the woman who continued to fellate the valet. "We miscalculated and her husband could not afford her. As for the male, his spouse does not want him. We shall sell them both elsewhere, of course."

The visitor bit his lower lip and thought swiftly. "Why shouldn't I just go to the authorities?"

"What authorities?" the Host replied with a laugh. "I am the authority here. Anyway, you don't even know the location of our island - it is one among thousands in this part of the world. Oh yes, apart from the cinematic record of your wife's wantonness, we also graphically recorded your exploits last night... the woman you enjoyed was someone's wife, of course. Finally, numbered among our patrons are the most powerful and ruthless people in the world. They would not thank you for risking their exposure to criminal charges."

"This is extortion!"

The man's wife toyed with her engorged nipples and stroked the surrounding silky flesh as she feverishly worked herself with her other hand.

"As you can see," the Host said, "she is particularly fond of those magnificent breasts. Her only aim is pleasure and she is fully-trained to satisfy your every whim."

The woman tossed her head back and groaned in the throes of a climax. Her husband suddenly noticed that he himself now had an erection.

"We offer a comprehensive after-sales service. She can be subjected to periodic refresher training. The discipline here is corporal and she probably would not wish to return more often than necessary."

"I cannot believe this," the visitor said. "I need time to think."

Spent now, shoulders relaxed, the woman stood obediently before the mirror and ran a hand through her dark mane.

"There is no shortage of alternative buyers. We have an offer for your wife already as a matter of fact - from the guest who had her last night. He is not a kind man and her bondage would not be easy. Our patrons include a wide spectrum of wealthy connoisseurs: minor European royalty, wealthy business people, Arab oil-sheiks, owners of specialist, high-class brothels ... we deal with anyone who has the money."

Now the major venue on the island - a cavernous, circular area in the main block of the complex. They called the large room the Big Hall. It was lavishly furnished, with every concession to fashionable and opulent design themes. Around the open, central dance floor, elegant wealthy people dined on the offerings of expert chefs. An orchestra played discreet music while guests drank fine wines and made sophisticated small talk.

Three women glided around the large room as if clad in expensive designer gowns. And a man, too, his naked cock erect and bobbing with each step. Leashed by fine chains affixed to their red collars, they were each led by a liveried valet. Guests watched appraisingly, comparing notes and exchanging comments.

The visitor, seated at a table towards the rear of the room, was again accompanied by two burly guards. He watched, clearly agonised. One of the women was his wife! A valet led her, placid and obedient, from one table to the next. She knelt on all fours as a man in Arab dress hefted her large, pendent breasts. Then someone parted her buttocks and she jerked as a finger invaded the exposed rear orifice.

Despite these indignities, she cooperated totally and without protest. A middle-aged, hard-faced woman cruelly pinched her inner thigh, and then sharply slapped her taut stomach. Someone forced her mouth widely open. She stood erect and passive as a large bearded man ran practised hands over her breasts, down her flanks, and then stood behind her, repeating the thorough appraisal. The naked woman meekly allowed him to lift each ankle and run his palm over the soles of her feet.

The valet tugged the leash and this beautiful, elegant woman progressed to the next table, smiling dutifully. There, a crone-like woman, expensively gowned and bejewelled, thrust two fingers deeply into the chattel's vagina. People at the table smiled when the painted hag commented on the cloying wetness she found there. Guards had warned the visitor to be silent. Several times he seemed about to jump to his feet but each time the valets restrained him. He watched grim-faced as his wife submitted to the degrading examinations.

"Enough," he said at last. "I will pay her price."

Carlos Fernandez, sitting alongside the Host, smiled with satisfaction.

"Congratulations," he said in his clipped Spanish accent. "Have you given any thought to the proposition I made regarding my own dear wife?"

The Host did not answer for some moments. Then he said: "Senor Fernandez, you are one of our most valued patrons, you have stocked your estate in Andalusia with purchases made here. Your wife - Serita, I believe? - participates in their discipline?"

"She is a cruel bitch with my women," Fernandez smiled, "but I would like experts to teach her."

"Very well. I will invite her to join our training team here. You must understand that you cannot hold me responsible for her fidelity. It is a sensuous island, as you are aware."

Fernandez laughed. "Our relationship has cooled to one of sexual indifference. There is one thing, though - Serita must not know that I have arranged this for her."

The Host inclined his head in agreement. "I will contact her without delay. As it happens, there will be fresh acquisitions for her to practise on, senor."

In London, on a cold morning in early summer, Sally Clark stepped from her apartment clad in running shoes, tiny shorts and a tight white vest that she particularly liked because it moulded so nicely against her ample breasts.

On that day, like any other, she set off to jog through the park, taking the same route and, as always, never speaking to a soul. Man-made hillocks and mown grass, thoughtfully planted shrubberies, metal bridges... she knew every twist and contour.

There were few people in the park at that time in the morning. An occasional workman taking a short-cut to one of the few remaining factories glanced up as she jogged past. Sometimes there would be a whistle of appreciation. There was some pleasure in that and, knowing herself appraised, she would suck in her gut, almost involuntarily accentuating her figure. Sally was an attractive young woman and, when skimpily clad in tight vest and running shorts, her charms were apparent enough.

Sally had lived alone ever since arriving in London after problems at home. Everything went well at first. She found a small but comfortable flat, albeit at an exorbitant rental. She even landed a job in the office of a solicitors' practice and commenced work, subject to satisfactory references. Then things began to go wrong. She never knew what her referees had written but, within weeks, the senior partner summoned her to his office... not quite what they wanted, best to part company now. As he spoke, the distinguished, steely-haired man had twisted a curiously-styled, iron signet ring on his finger.

It proved almost impossible to find another job. Sally's money was dwindling fast and her rent was in arrears. Then, quite unexpectedly, she met the urbane senior solicitor, her ex-boss, near her apartment block. He seemed quite concerned about her welfare and gave her a business card, advising that she contact the person named. She did so and now, two months later, found herself working for an escort agency.

At least, that was what it was politely called. Like all of the other girls at the agency, Sally discovered that it was easy to supplement the meagre pay by offering extra services. Many assignments ended in bed in some hotel room. She told herself that it was not prostitution. Not really. And always, but always, Sally rose in the early hours and returned to her own apartment, determined to keep some semblance of normality in her life.

On this particular day, workmen seemed to be repairing the track again. They had parked a large yellow van on the grass and deep muddy tracks showed where it had been driven from the nearby roadway. Its rear-doors were open, with a metal ramp at the rear for unloading and loading from the tailgate. Two men clad in blue donkey-jackets leaned on spades some yards from the van, in the very centre of the path.

Accustomed to frank stares and lewd comments from workmen, Sally jogged past but stared straight ahead and ran onto the muddy grass to skirt the two men. However, this was not just another dull morning. She had scarcely passed the workmen when they grabbed her arms, a man on either side. Without giving her a chance to break stride, before she could even scream, they ran her up the ramp and into the van. Before she knew what was happening the men applied a fetid pad to her face, and she lost consciousness almost immediately.

Jade Preston, naked, padded into the large bedroom of her London home, glancing instinctively at the full-length mirror as she passed. She was never missed the opportunity to view her image and she was usually pleased by what she saw. She wandered across the room to open the uppermost drawer of a dressing table, the drawer filled with the expensive frothy lingerie that she adored. Then, suddenly aware that eyes were upon her, she turned and saw her husband, watching from the doorway. He was clad in a black silk dressing gown.

"John! You startled me," she said with a smile, straightening and enjoying his frank stare. "When did you get back?"

"I arrived in the early hours - didn't want to wake you. Have you been good?"

"Very good, I think," she said with a wicked smile. "How was your trip?"

"It was profitable. Come here..."

She approached him and moulded herself against his hard body, shivering at the deliciously sensuous feel of soft silk against her naked curves. "Darling," she wheedled, "would you mind if Sebastian joined us for the cruise next week?"

"You have been seeing him again?"

"Well, yes." Jade nuzzled her lips against his neck. "You said you wouldn't mind."

Jade felt him straighten slightly. Her heart pounded a little for, tolerant as John was about her peccadillos, she suspected that there were limits. But then, their marriage was supposed to be open and modern.

Jade had always been a sensuous creature. She needed men. John, tanned and handsome, was the nearest she had found to her ideal partner. He had an air of mystery and danger about him. Jade knew instinctively that many of his jaunts overseas involved some risk but John never said anything about that. He was a strong and self-assured man and it was this strength that Jade found attractive. But he was away from home so often...

"What do you see in that pretty boy?"

"I don't know," she confessed.

She spoke the truth: Jade did not truly know what she sought in love or sex. No matter how good her relationship with John, no matter how many casual affairs, there was always something missing. Oh, she found sexual satisfaction of a sort but there was something indefinable and extra that she yearned for. Perhaps, that was why she was always exploring her own sexuality.

John reached down to stroke her fleecy cleft, quickly finding the unusually large and protuberant clitoris that nestled there. Jade squirmed as she felt the nub becoming massively engorged. That little monster between her sex lips always forced her to yield to strong base appetites, the ones she did not properly understand.

He hurled her upon the bed. Jade liked it that way. A warm glow heated her belly. She wanted him to maul her small pert breasts. She needed to feel small and helpless beneath his power. Once charged with passion, Jade was voracious in demanding penetration, and her heart palpitated as he bludgeoned his rampant penis into her wet slit and she bucked up to receive it. Groans and ecstatic cries filled the room as he pistoned violently within the yielding, fully-awakened feminine flesh.

John was a capable and virile lover. His violent fucking went on for some time. Then, when Jade was reduced to a quivering, begging animal, his forefinger found the rose of her anus. God! she loved that. This was always the supreme moment. Jade bucked and writhed as he penetrated the tight opening and, within seconds, a deep, throaty gurgle announced the onslaught of her climax. Presently, panting and perspiring, she lay beside him on the bed.

"You don't have to invite Sebastian on the cruise if you don't want to," she said.

"There's room on the boat."

"Sebastian isn't strong, you know. Not like you. Neither am I."

John did not reply as he rose from the bed and pulled the dressing gown over his shoulders. Rather than looking into his face, Jade gazed at his semi-tumescent cock, framed as it was by the open drape of black silk.

"I did not expect you back so soon," she said. "Sebastian was going to take me to the theatre this evening."

"That's okay. One of the Foreign Office boys has arranged a business meeting for me tonight. I'll be in Soho at a place called the Bond-Age Club."

CHAPTER TWO

Outwardly, The Bond-Age Club was just a dimly lit and shabby clip-joint with a cynical SM theme. It was typical of such seedy establishments that are to be found in every capital around the world.

The Host quietly observed the scene from his vantage point in a gloomy corner of the basement room. An acceptable number of customers enjoyed the company of scantily-clad young men and women at the various tables. Everything seemed to be in order. He heard Felix Tranter, one of the patrons that night, speaking loudly and angrily in a guttural American accent. Tranter's companions - two burly, thuggish-looking fellows - made feeble attempts to mollify him.

A deferential waitress approached the Host, carrying a tray. She was scantily clad in a leather and chain harness and a black G-string. Trembling hands betrayed the woman's anxiety. She proffered her quivering naked breasts invitingly near to his face when stooping to collect an empty glass. The Host waved her away but the woman leaned forward again to whisper in his ear. Nodding, he rose in his own time, glass in hand, and wandered to tap on the door at the rear of the basement room.

"Yes?"

"It is the Host."

Security bolts were withdrawn and the door opened. The Host was familiar with the layout; he walked down a corridor to an office without acknowledging the doorkeeper. The atmosphere and décor here were wholly different to the dismal surroundings in the club room: understated elegance with a distinctly opulent feel. A woman clad in a smart business suit quickly rose to greet him but her eyes were studiously downcast. Although her clothing was outwardly austere, underneath the suit, he knew, she would be naked.

Anyone could quickly unfasten her white blouse, which buttoned at the front, and, although supported, her breasts would be uncovered beneath. They could easily hitch up the loose, flared skirt about her waist. There would be no knickers, nothing to obstruct access to her intimacies. He knew all of this. After all, the woman wore his ring; the shield-shaped iron signet, inlaid with gold, showed a many-spoked wheel set within an outer circle. It was a sign. Such women were duty-bound to choose clothing that could be easily thrust aside.

"Tranter is the large American with the toupee?" the Host asked, eying her from head to toe.

12

"Yes, sir. He has been waiting some time and getting rather angry."

The Host shrugged. He did not care. "Send a couple of girls to his table. I will look at the figures."

"Mr Tranter is -"

"Tranter can cool his heels for a while."

The Host sat at a computer, studying the income and expenditure of the Bond-Age Club. Lily paced back and forth but remained deferentially silent. He knew she was nervous and he enjoyed that. Glancing up, he appraised the woman cooly. Although nearly forty years old, she was still attractive, he thought. Expertly applied cosmetics helped of course, but her body was good, too.

After thirty minutes or so, the Host switched off the PC and rose to his feet. He meaningfully patted Lily's rounded rump and a surge of desire coursed his body when he felt her quake. His gesture was unmistakable. In immediate response, without demur, Lily lay upon the polished surface of the desk, atop papers and stationery. He thrust the loose skirt beyond her midriff, revealing a black corset and below, between the garter straps, a neatly-trimmed triangle of silky black hair. The Host took her swiftly, almost brutally. When he was done, she fastened her clothing without murmuring a word.

Returning to the dimly-lit club room, The Host walked ponderously towards the table where the large red-haired American sat with a couple of burly, thuggish-looking men and two delectable young women.

"Mr Tranter, I believe?"

"About time - I don't like waiting around. Sit, we have business."

The Host instinctively disliked the American. He raised his eyebrows quizzically and dismissed the two women with a gesture of his head before taking a seat at the table.

"What is the nature of our business?"

"This is a good setup. A bit run-down but okay. I am in the market for places like this."

"It is not for sale."

"Everything is for sale."

"Not the Bond-Age Club."

"That could be rough."

The Host smiled mirthlessly. He held the man's eyes for long moments and then said quietly: "I fear you have had a long wait for a very short meeting, Mr Tranter. Do not meddle in things you cannot understand. Get out!"

Tranter's jaw dropped slightly and his oafish henchmen hesitated. The Host, seemingly utterly confident, maintained a hard, unflinching stare and presently Tranter laughed and rose to his feet. "OK, so we play it your way. I hope you know what you are doing."

After the men left, the Host gestured towards to a waitress. As he took the proffered glass, the house-lights dimmed further and a statuesque young woman appeared on the small stage, apparently supervised by a whip-wielding bare chested man. The Host critically watched her routine as she cavorted and stripped to a wild rhythm, writhing away from the curling whip. He could tell that the young woman was aware of his presence and he was pleased that her fear gave an added edge to the performance. She was soon stark naked and kneeling suppliantly before the whip. Then the music changed and the woman threw herself into the sinuous, erotic floor movements of a captured slave. She was a fine testament to the organisation's training methods.

The Host glowered when a stranger sauntered casually across the room to sit uninvited at his table.

"She's very good," the newcomer said, casually turning to look at the writhing woman. "I have a gun under the table, pointing directly at your groin."

"Really?" The Host's calm voice did not betray the pang of fear that gripped him.

The other smiled coldly as he revealed the briefest glimpse of a small handgun. "Finish your drink and then walk quietly towards the exit."

Suddenly, without warning, the threatened man overturned the table. He heard a loud report from the gun; the assassin had not been bluffing. There was a sharp, sickening pain in his right arm. He looked down and saw blood seeping through the sleeve of his jacket. He heard the stripper scream as she fled the stage and he was aware of other patrons leaping to their feet in panic. Even in those fleeting moments, the Host expected the next shot and oblivion. Then the gunman was on the ground, struggling beneath a lithe young man who had leapt to grapple with him. The Host staggered back as the gunman managed to scramble free and fled the basement room.

"Are you injured?" the rescuer asked, smoothing his hair.

"A flesh wound, I think."

"Do you know that person?"

"Not yet." The Host nursed his wounded arm grimly. "I am in your debt, Mr...?"

"Preston. My name is John Preston."

"You are remarkably calm, sir, considering the circumstances."

Preston shrugged and gave a slight smile. "Look," he said, "you should call the police."

"No!"

Lily appeared from the rooms at the rear, ashen-faced. The Host smiled thinly. He knew that she feared recall and punishment - they euphemistically termed it refresher training. Hurriedly, Lily ushered the Host to the private rooms and seated him at her desk as she fumbled with a first-aid box. "I'm sorry, sir, but -"

"Just get my arm cleaned up. I want a full report on Tranter and his associates. A full report, Lily. Is that clear?"

"Yes sir," she said, bathing the wound with an antiseptic solution.

"Oh, and get one of the girls to look after the young man who saved my life. His name is Preston, John Preston. Ouch."

"I'm sorry," Lily stammered as he flinched.

"Get Preston's address and run a report on him too. I always pay my debts, Lily." He winced in pain, clenching and unclenching the hand of his damaged arm. "No problems with the new acquisitions?"

Lily shook her head. "Good fresh stock ... safely packed and transported yesterday. They should have reached the island by now."

"Do not look any one of us in the face," the Head Valet ordered, swishing a leather whip. Sally Clark immediately averted her eyes and stared submissively at the ground. "It is the beginning. There is only one rule, and that is to obey every rule. You own nothing - neither hands, breasts nor any orifice. They are ours. You must never touch any intimate part of your bodies. Always in our presence you must keep your legs apart. You will display your bodies as we command and submit to any touch or usage."

The captives - nine of them, including three men - had been snatched with ruthless efficiency and transported via freight aircraft and boat to this strange place, and they were still in a state of shock. They all seemed as bewildered as Sally by this strangely-clad fellow who wore a red fitted jacket, white frilled shirt, breeches, white stockings and buckled shoes. The man saw Sally looking at him and she quickly averted her eyes, anxious not to invite further unwelcome attention. Yet still she could feel his appraising stare and the young woman standing next to her moaned, a curious mewing sound.

Sally huddled among the other captives beside the wall of a large circular building that nestled against the mountain side. She had been horrified by the sight of nude men and women degradingly bound and displayed in the gardens, tied in cruel positions, merely, it seemed, for ornamentation. The other captives had seen them too, of course, and they were scarcely less apprehensive. It was an early indication of what lay in store for them. And, indeed, the valets had allowed the newcomers neither modesty nor privacy.

Like the others, Sally had stripped upon command, quickly, for the valets carried many-thonged whips and they were not against using them. She had been acutely embarrassed as they eyed her nudity so openly.

The captives showered under supervision, men and women together, washing the grime and sweat of long journeys from their flesh. Each of them, Sally thought, was quite beautiful: the women had good breasts and smooth skin, while the men were well-muscled, athletic and very handsome. A doc-

15

tor gave each one a medical examination, an exhaustive and humiliating ordeal under the eyes of their captors, and all were pronounced medically fit. Now they stood, utterly naked, before the Head Valet - a man of some authority, evidently.

"In the quarantine cells you will be nude and, sometimes, blindfolded," he went on. "When free people visit you, you must do as they demand, although you will not serve them fully until your health is confirmed. When a valet or guest requires it, you will simply open or pull aside their clothing and close it again when he or she is done with you.

"The valets will whip you frequently, every day, neither in punishment nor just because we wish it but for your instruction. Besides that, if you incur our displeasure, you will receive additional beatings. The valets will frequently attend you and always before they extinguish the lights to confine you upon your beds. You will now be processed and shown to your cells."

Was he mad, Sally asked herself? She remembered how she had already received a sharp lesson in discipline, feeling the biting lashes of a valet's whip about her thighs. It was not pleasant. A man held the door widely open and the frightened victims passed through, taking care to keep their eyes downcast. Inside, they were hurried down into a basement. Two more valets waited there.

"Stand in line," the Head Valet ordered.

They all stood completely naked, awkward and embarrassed under the valets' scrutiny. Sally belatedly remembered to spread her thighs and received a sharp crack across quivering buttocks for her tardiness. Her scream was a timely reminder for the others, and they all hastily widened their legs even further.

"Stand straight. Hands up high. Keep your feet spread. You" - he tapped Sally with his whip - "step forward."

Sally reluctantly uncrossed her arms and slowly raised her hands aloft, holding them high on either side of her head. There was no escape. Her nude body fully displayed, she moved to stand before the valet. It was almost unreal to her: she stood meekly, as if in a daze, as the man fixed a stiff leather strap around her neck. The broad band was uncomfortable and it forced her chin up high. Then they locked leather bracelets about each of her wrists. Finally, humiliatingly, the valet cupped her right breast in his hand and made a mark there with a black grease crayon that was slick against her soft flesh. She shuddered involuntarily.

Then they led her to a stout support pillar. Perhaps a locked collar does something to a woman, for she was numbly compliant as the valet clipped her wrists to hooks above her head. Sally heard the gasps of watching slaves before she felt the first excruciating, searing pain across her back. Half-turning in utter shock, she saw the Head Valet swinging his whip again and her mouth half-opened to scream. He was deliberate and thorough, calculating the timing of his blows and always striking at writhing buttocks and thighs.

She screeched and begged for mercy as the leather repeatedly bit into her flesh. The pain was intolerable, yet amid it all there was something else: a strange, disquieting sensation in her belly. Perhaps it was the ritual of enslavement - the enforced nudity before her captors, the collaring - she did not know.

As the whip bit, as she squirmed desperately, wrapping her legs about the stout, unyielding pillar, Sally Clark experienced a tumultuous orgasm that completely overwhelmed her. Thank God neither the Head Valet nor his men, nor the other captives, had noticed. When finally released from the pillar, Sally swooned and would have collapsed to the ground had a valet not held her.

"Next," shouted the Head Valet and through half-closed eyes Sally saw a young man, ashen and trembling, step forward to receive his collar. Another valet knelt to secure a small harness around the man's thickly erect shaft.

She saw no more of what they did to him. A valet ushered her, still naked, through an arched entrance at the rear of the basement. In the narrow tunnel beyond, despite the fresh whitewash, it was dark and gloomy. The tunnel was inadequately lit by bare electric light bulbs but she could see that it slowly wound round, perhaps in a complete circle. Within the perimeter, stone walls, arranged as in the spokes of a wheel, geometrically divided the vaults. These walls, radiating from the centre, obviously supported the large rotunda-like building above. This created several segment-shaped recesses, each extending to a point somewhere in the gloom at the hub of the circular structure. Stout bars curved around the outer arcs, some twelve feet across, fronting the tunnelled walkway and converting each segment into a secure cell.

None of the pens were individually lit but some illumination came from bare lamps strung around the outer tunnel. Sally saw that many cells held a naked prisoner. There were more women, nude and svelte, than hard muscled men. Some cowered away from the bars, as if seeking to hide in the shadowy gloom. None showed any pity as the valet led the newcomer past their cells. An occupant could only see the few feet of winding tunnel that extended on either side of her own cage.

"Halt," the valet ordered, pushing Sally against the bars of an unoccupied enclosure some way around the tunnel. He unlocked the barred gate and thrust her into the cell. She fell onto a rough palliasse upon a wooden platform and lay there while the man chained her wrists to a ring that was set in the wall. Then he passed his gloved hand roughly between her thighs. She was wet there. The valet glanced at the damp patch on his glove and smiled knowingly. Sally blushed and hid her head.

"Keep yourself open there," he reminded her before locking the gate and striding away.

It took a considerable amount of time for the valets to collar, mark and whip all of the new acquisitions. From the sleeping platform where they had chained her, Sally watched the nude wretches weep as they passed the cell - yes, the men, too - their bodies warmed and striped by the Head Valet's whip.

Meanwhile, back in the Bond-Age Club, London...

The Policeman smiled wanly at the bare-breasted waitress as he accepted a glass of whisky. Lily shrugged an apology when he grimaced at the taste of the insipid liquor.

"I have told you all I know," she said, nervously glancing over her shoulder.

"Yes, yes." He handed her a large brown envelope. "These are the reports you need. It's all in there, a complete run-down on Felix Tranter and information about John Preston."

"The Host would have me killed if it is ever discovered that these reports are false."

The policeman smiled as he rose to leave. "Do keep in touch," he said.

"The reports will be on the Host's desk by tomorrow," Lily promised.

CHAPTER THREE

A masked nude stood beside the Host's desk, statue-like, hip turned, right leg flexed and toes pointed. The naked woman's magnificent breasts were thrust forward and taut muscles constricted her trim waist. Flesh surrounding the high, swollen slit of her sex had been shaven. The ornate mask entirely encased her head: black, sequined velvet embellished with a confection of purple, green and yellow feathers. This curious headgear denied sight, sound and hearing to the wearer. A prim woman clad in functional business clothes attended to the administrative work. She seemed to disdain, even ignore, the masked nude.

The Host's injury had proved to be nothing more than a minor inconvenience and he was quickly back at work. It was a wound to his pride more than to his flesh. Still, the incident had provided a salutary lesson: he would be more careful in future. •

"Next business."

"This is the special file you ordered on John Preston."

The Host eagerly took the folder and idly flicked through its pages. This was good! It had not taken long since the incident at the Bond Age Club.

"An international arms dealer!" he said, surprised. "Any foreseeable problems?"

"None," the secretary replied, handing him some large, glossy photographs. "That's his wife."

The Host studied the prints with some satisfaction: the young woman was obviously photogenic. He would enjoy the day when Jade Preston wore his mask! "This one is very special to me," he said.

"May I ask why, Sir?"

"No. Just acquire her. Next."

"This is the other report received from Lily."

"Excellent!"

The Host suppressed his delight when the secretary suddenly reached forward to cruelly pinch one of the masked nude's long brown nipples. He enjoyed the way the unfortunate woman jerked forward and tensed, anticipating another nip.

"Really!" he said in mock rebuke.

"I was just checking our confidentiality, Sir."

"She is unable to see or hear, I assure you."

The Host caressed the nude's silky buttocks. She again nervously leapt beneath his unexpected touch. He was particularly pleased with the head-dress, for it allowed him to decorate his office while engaged in the most sensitive work. Invariably, at some time during a work-session, he would surprise the woman allotted to the mask that day, using her roughly and mercilessly. However, on this morning, the Host relished his work. He was content to make the masked nude wait in fearful anticipation, blind and dumb, hearing nothing. He knew from experience that in such circumstances, the slightest touch, particularly on sensitised erogenous zones, caused a woman's body to leap involuntarily.

Back to business, he thought. Quickly, he scanned the report, muttering to himself. "Felix Tranter... New York. Fortune based on criminal activities... capable and ruthless. Has extensive commercial interests in the former Soviet Union. Ah, married to a former Olympic gymnast!" He looked up at the secretary, tapping the papers. "Acquire Natasha Tranter!"

The secretary nodded without showing any surprise as she made a quick note.

"Jade Preston and Natasha Tranter. I will organise it, Sir," she said briskly, turning to leave the room.

Less than a week later. Moscow. The towering, dark and gloomy Intourist Hotel. Natasha Tranter petulantly slammed a bottle of expensive Parisian perfume against the wall, shattering it into a hundred shards.

"It's a rat-hole. I swear I saw a cockroach in the bathroom."

"This is Moscow, honey," her husband protested. "It's the best they have."

"It is not! Even in the days of the Party they had better hotels. This is for scumbags. You, the important Western businessman... Bah!"

"I'm sorry, baby," Felix crooned soothingly. "We are only here for a couple of days. I'll make sure the accommodation is better in Siberia. Give me a smile, uh?"

"Siberia! You imbecile. Do you think they have five-star hotels in Siberia?"

As it turned out, the accommodation in Novosibirsk, capital of Western Siberia, was better than the grim Moscow hotel. They lodged in an apartment complex sited beside a huge man-made reservoir, providing magnificent panoramic views. The old Soviet regime had euphemistically called the place a sanatorium and people still knew it as such. Actually, it had always been a well-equipped and rather plush health centre where privileged Party officials spent their family holidays. Things were little different now; corrupt and powerful local barons still had exclusive use of the holiday centre - usually the same individuals as before, who had simply transferred their power-base. These people were keen to do business with the powerful and equally crooked American and they provided him with the best they had to offer.

The summer climate was surprisingly pleasant and, while Felix Tranter went off to explore devious business-deals, Natasha was kept amused with excursions into the surrounding countryside. Lazy boat trips up the huge River Ob, visits to traditional Siberian peasant villages... it was, she found to her surprise, wonderfully beautiful. Her native language returned to fluency and she began to enjoy herself. A significant factor in this was the company of her handsome young guide, a lively and amusing Muscovite with a quick laugh.

Sasha had other talents besides linguistic ability. He and Natasha writhed together in the forest on a bed of pine needles, rolled in soft hay in a village barn, thrashed about on a bed in a riverside dacha... Natasha's strong sexual appetites matched Sasha's youthful virility.

"Where are you taking me now?" she asked Sasha as the Trans-Siberian Express lumbered to a stop at Novosibirsk railway station.

"Ah, a surprise!"

After sailing for a few hours in the windy Aegean Sea, the Prestons had anchored their small yacht in a sheltered, idyllic cove where crystalline waters glistened. Jade rose from a lounger and adjusted the one piece swimsuit about her trim buttocks. She looked down at the invitingly clear water.

"John," she called. "I'm going for a swim. Care to join me?"

"That's too energetic."

"What about you, Seb?"

"Sure," said the tanned young man who was lounging in a net hammock.

Jade watched him rise to his feet and languidly stretch to display large biceps and a trim, rippling body. He was clad in a tiny white thong. She knew that many thought Sebastian to be a slightly foppish young man. Yes, she thought, as he padded across the deck, there is something about him that makes one wonder, but he is good in bed with his large wide cock. She pushed these thoughts from her mind, aware that John was watching as Seb dived from the deck in a graceful, arching swoop that barely caused a ripple on the water's surface. With a laugh and a wave to her husband, Jade plunged into the sea after him.

They swam strongly away. After some time, pausing for breath and treading water, Jade took stock of her bearings. The yacht was some distance away and land was even further. She smiled widely and clasped Seb, gluing her lips to his.

Suddenly, her ankles were firmly grasped. At the same time, Sebastian seemed to sink away from her. Strong hands were tugging her relentlessly beneath the surface. Jade struggled desperately, swallowing water, trying to kick out, but she felt herself being inexorably pulled to a lower depth. When her lungs felt as if they were about to implode, blackness overcame her.

21

At first nobody on the yacht worried at Jade's prolonged absence. Both Sebastian and Jade were accomplished swimmers. After some thirty minutes, John Preston became anxious and he scanned the seascape using binoculars. A glance at the skipper's charts showed that there were no small islands in the vicinity, certainly not within swimming distance. When an hour had elapsed, everyone on board began to panic. The skipper cruised the boat around the bay but they could not see either Jade or Seb.

Later, the distraught Preston reported their loss to a policeman on the island of Naxos. The authorities mounted a halfhearted search but, as the policeman said, there were some unexpectedly dangerous currents in the area and the bodies could have been swept out to sea.

Jade Preston awakened to the sound of a throbbing engine. She was alone. The surroundings were strange and alien. Gradually, her thoughts cleared: swimming, the tug on her legs from below, something covering her face...

She was on a small boat and it was moving, the motion told her that. So someone had rescued her! Thank God! Where was Seb?

Rising from the bunk, she went to try the handle of the cabin door.

Locked!

"Hello," Jade called.

No reply.

She banged on the polished wood, softly at first and then harder when there was no answer, until it hurt her small clenched fist. Cold and shivering, she returned to sit upon the bunk, crossing her arms and clasping her shoulders. How long had she been unconscious? It must have been quite a time because the black material of her swimming costume was almost dry now and marked with white salt stains. But the bunk was slightly damp; clearly, someone had lain her wet unconscious body upon it. There was no blanket or sheet, nothing to wrap around her. Then she heard someone descending the steps outside and the door opened. A tall young man clad only in brief white shorts ducked his head as he entered.

"Hello," she said, smiling and rising. "I guess I have to thank you for saving my life."

He ignored her proffered handshake and made no reply. She blanched and crossed her arms before his frank gaze.

"There was a man with me in the water..."

"He is safe."

"Thank God. Where are we?"

"The sea," he replied in his thick accent.

"I'm very cold. Is there any clothing on board?"

The man merely gestured that she should leave the cabin. His manner was disquieting and strange. She blinked upon emerging into the bright sunlight but welcomed the warming rays. It was, she saw, a small ocean-

22

going fishing vessel and Jade saw Scuba gear laid upon a hatch. An older, weather-beaten man stood at the wheel.

"The lovely Mrs Preston!" he called. "You are awake."

"You know my name?"

"How are you feeling?"

"Cold!"

The younger man stepped forward, grasping the top of her costume and yanking it down to her waist. Jade gasped in horror and astonishment. In turning, she saw Sebastian, who lay crouched on his side, hog-tied. He was naked.

"What the hell are you doing?" she yelled at the deckhand, hastily pulling the clinging material back over her breasts.

"You must learn to obey, quickly and without question," the man at the wheel said. "There is always a punishment for disobedience."

Then Jade heard herself scream as a searing pain spread across her thighs. Turning in shock, mouth agape and eyes wide, she was amazed to see that the young man held a cane.

"Hold out your hand," he ordered, raising the cane.

It was outrageous!

"Do as he says," the skipper called. "Your punishment will double each time you refuse. And you will find the cane preferable across the palm of your hand rather than on your bare arse."

"Why?" she stammered, flinching at the obscenity.

"Four strokes."

Jade was about to protest again but she thought better of it. Numbly, she held out her right hand, palm uppermost, biting her lower lip like a naughty child. The cane stung ferociously and she yelped each time it struck. Afterwards, she rubbed her hands vigorously, tears welling in her eyes.

"Now - the swimsuit."

With a groan of defeat, Jade turned away and slowly tugged the fabric down, revealing her bare breasts again. She looked up but the skipper made a gesture. Her heart sank further but there was no mistaking his meaning. Her fingers pushed the tight garment over her hips and thighs and she allowed it to fall around her ankles.

"Bring it to me."

Jade stooped to disentangle it from her feet and took it the skipper.

"Thank you," he said, tossing the garment into the sea.

Jade was acutely aware of the man's eyes upon her naked body. "Are you going to rape me?" she asked.

"You must only speak when invited. You are under the strictest discipline. We will punish transgressions. Lower your hands." Jade allowed her arms to drop to her sides. She stood awkwardly before him. "Lie on the deck, here, on your back." He paused as she fearfully obeyed. "Open your

23

legs. Wider. Flex your knees. Hands by your side, palms up. Good. Stay."

Splayed as she was, womanhood opened, Jade knew that her large clitoris would be prominently displayed, for it protruded even when dormant. Now, despite herself, the nub was becoming engorged and protuberant. The treacherous appendage positively invited investigation. However, neither of the men made any move towards her. Jade shuddered, knowing that Seb would be viewing her gaping sex from his crouched position on the deck.

Hardly daring to move a muscle, she closed her eyes to shut out the image of the captain. She was to remain prone, the sun warming her body, for about twenty minutes. Then they commanded her to roll onto her belly, legs still splayed. Even as she lay on the pitching deck, frightened and confused, the engine vibrated the deck timbers and caused a relentless tingling sensation centred upon her throbbing clitoris.

"Get up!"

A further twenty minutes had passed. She rose to her feet, stumbling a little.

"You'll find wine and food in the galley. Go down and fix a meal for us all. You are not to eat until given permission."

The blond man led Jade to the galley and left her to her own devices. Grimacing at the grease and grime, she tentatively opened cupboards and drawers. Knives! Taking a large, sharp meat-cleaver, she hefted it experimentally. For fleeting moments her spirits were uplifted but then grim reality dawned. Neither she nor Sebastian was a sailor. How would they manage the boat? There was no land in sight. She had no idea of their geographical location. Their plight was hopeless and she replaced the cleaver in a drawer.

Jade found the food and grudgingly prepared a simple meal. Minutes later, she emerged on deck carrying a salad bowl and cutting board, with an icy cold wine bottle tucked under her arm, chilling her naked flesh.

"You learn quickly."

"Can I untie my friend?"

Again the cane seared across her thighs and Jade realised that she had spoken without permission. Seb looked up pathetically and she hung her head. They sent her back to the galley to thoroughly clean the area. Fearing the cane, Jade applied herself diligently as she knelt, scrubbing the floor with a hard brush. Her heart beat heavily when the blond man came to check on her work, cane in hand. When he nodded his approval, she almost sank to her knees in gratitude. Then the man locked her in the small cabin. She saw that he had placed a rough blanket on the bunk and she wrapped it around her gratefully.

She had no idea how long she remained there. The monotonous throb of the engines, the steady rolling of the small craft, and the sheer weight of events that day lulled her into a restless sleep.

Later, the young man wakened her and roughly pulled away the blanket. He tossed it onto the bunk and, grasping her hair so that she was bent low, led her back on deck. Seb was now sitting miserably on his haunches, hands still tied to his ankles. His large limp cock drooped between spread legs.

"Kneel," the young man told Jade thrusting her head towards the scrubbed planks. She went down on all fours beside a pale of soapy water placed there. "Sit back on your heels. Head high."

He began to lave suds into her hair, working his fingers through her tresses to produce thick soapy lather. The young man then ordered Jade back onto all fours, her head pressed down upon the deck and buttocks raised, knees apart.

The next touch was unexpected and her body leapt. His slippery finger slicked around her clitoris, teasing it into almost immediate erection. He laughed. Jade steeled herself as the young man - perhaps no more than seventeen years of age - thoroughly washed her intimacies, using the leathery palms of his hands. He probed and massaged lather into the lips of her sex and she let out a small grunt when the tips of his fingers invaded her vagina.

"Ease back onto my fingers," he ordered.

Jade went rigid. He picked up the cane with his free hand and tapped it against her thigh. Groaning inwardly, she obeyed, tentatively rocking back onto the invading digits. The soapy fingers slipped in and out of her cleft with ease. Then it was over. The man calmly withdrew his fingers and applied more lather to her body. He made her stand, legs apart and with hands clasped behind her head. When she turned, Jade saw that Seb's cock had grown hard. Her humiliation excited him!

Docilely, she allowed the deckhand to wash her naked body, massaging his hands over breasts, flanks, belly, thighs and feet. When finished, he did not allow her to break position. She stood gasping as the man lashed pails of cold water over her body, rinsing away the suds.

She was left like that for the remainder of the journey: standing erect, hands behind her head, legs widely apart, the clearly discernible head of her clitoris pink amid a nest of silky dark hair. She stood as she must, facing the warm wind, her breasts thrust forward, nipples protuberant from recent attentions and the caress of the wind.

"Now you," she heard the young deckhand say, reaching for Seb.

"No!"

The cane lashed across Sebastian's shoulders and the deckhand grinned. He pulled the naked man to his knees and Sebastian crouched there with his back bowed by the hog-tie. Glancing from the corner of her eye, Jade saw that the man similarly lathered Seb and thoroughly washed him.

"Ease back."

Seb, undoubtedly afraid of the cane, did not protest, but Jade heard his cry of anguish. Then a slight grunt. Jade knew that the deckhand's probing fingers had penetrated Seb's body. She could see Seb, his back bowed and buttocks upraised, with head against the deck boards. Then the deckhand produced a knife and reached down with it between Seb's legs, where his large balls hung. She held her breath.

Laughing, the deckhand drew back and cut the tether that trussed the captive's hands and ankles together. He was still bound hand and foot but could at least straighten now. The man dragged him to his feet and Jade saw that Seb's large thick cock was very hard and erect now. She heard him gasp as a pail of icy water was upturned above his head.

When she was dry, the young deckhand tossed Jade a simple tunic, fashioned from a single piece of white cotton and tied with a belt of similar material. The garment was very short, scarcely covering the rise of her buttocks, and slashed to the waist so that it almost revealed her breasts. As for Seb, they merely fashioned a tiny white apron that draped incongruously over his erect penis.

The Skipper ordered Jade to resume an upright stance, with her legs spread and hands clasped behind her neck. She was aware that her upraised arms lifted the wind-tugged hem of the tunic even further up her body, perhaps even revealing the fleece of her mound. Land came into sight within another few minutes. Jade knew that she and Seb, scandalously clad and obviously under strict discipline, presented onlookers with a fine sight when the boat moored at the jetty of a remote, rocky island. She dare not move until given permission to do so and Sebastian, too, was utterly submissive.

Mrs Jade Preston stepped awkwardly onto the jetty from the bobbing rowing boat. Another man, clad in a strange red and black livery awaited her. Seb, was lying on the boards. "Who is in charge here?" she demanded, her courage returning.

"I am the Head Valet," the man said. Then, pointing at Seb, he asked the skipper, "Who is this?"

"He was with her. We couldn't take one without the other."

The Head Valet roughly hauled Seb onto the jetty. He looked at the young man's bulging muscles and trim, tanned body. "Could be a nice bonus," he conceded.

The cold, dismissive tone told Jade that she could expect little help from this man. She looked about her, shielding her eyes against the sun. A rocky mountain towered behind the small cluster of whitewashed buildings that nestled on the waterfront. There were people there. Civilisation! She sprinted wildly up the causeway.

"These men have kidnapped me. Help."

Jade ran from one person to another. Two fishermen were mending their nets but they merely shrugged before returning to their labours. A taverna sprawled towards the water's edge; two old men, busy playing backgammon, angrily brushed her away. Four or five younger men, seated at a table, merely laughed and exchanged ribald comments in what Jade took to be Greek.

"Fools. My husband is very wealthy - he will reward you."

The Head Valet sauntered to stand beside her, smiling as he said, "That was very silly."

"Help me," Jade wept. "Please!"

At that point a young woman appeared from the shade of the taverna, bearing a tray laden with bottles and drinking-glasses. Jade gasped: not only was the woman quite naked, she was also chained. A long leash trailed from the green collar around her neck, secured to a point inside the taverna and trailing behind her as she walked; her wrists, too, were manacled and connected by, perhaps, eighteen inches of light, silver chain. The naked waitress smiled shyly as she passed.

The Head Valet did not allow Jade to dwell upon this, for he immediately grasped her hair and bent her over a nearby table. Her cheek was pressed against the warm wooden slats. Then she yelped with shock as fiery pain scorched across her thighs. The short tunic rode up over bare her buttocks and another stripe from the swishing thongs bit into the quivering flesh.

"No!" she screamed, her legs kicking out. "Take your hands off me, you bastard."

Resistance was useless. Jade gripped the edges of the table in fury as the viciously-stinging lashes switched across her tender flesh. Finally, sobbing uncontrollably and thoroughly chastised, Jade remained prone, her tear-soaked cheek upon the rough table. Her bottom felt as though it was on fire. She saw that the naked waitress scarcely glanced at her as she returned into the taverna.

"Come," the Head Valet said. "The Doctor will examine you."

"They call me simply the Doctor. This lady is the Nurse. Remove your clothing."

Jade Preston now neither expected nor received any concession to modesty. She stood naked, feeling shamed before the three clothed strangers. A valet reached forward to remove the ropes that bound Seb, and cut the twine to allow the small ragged apron to flutter away from the captive's now dormant cock. Jade saw Seb glance uneasily towards her.

The Doctor's medical centre was surprisingly well-equipped and his examination was thorough. For the next hour or so her body was subjected to a battery of tests. The Doctor raised his eyebrows upon discovering the large fleshy clitoris that protruded from between her leaf-like lips, but he made no comment. Samples were required and duly provided. Numbed by

27

recent experiences, Jade silently suffered the indignities of the probing, intimate examination. Then she waited, sitting disconsolately on a high trolley, with hands clasped about her knees, while the Doctor wrote comprehensive notes.

"Have you ever contracted a sexually transmitted disease?"

Jade hesitated and then admitted, "Yes, a minor infection."

More questions followed: childhood illnesses, sleep patterns, diet. Each time Jade answered, The Doctor nodded and made more notes.

Presently, the valet asked: "Okay?"

"Yes," the Doctor said closing his file. "Fit for anything, as far as I can tell. Strict quarantine, of course."

With that, the valet grasped Jade's upper forearm and hauled her from the table. She glanced fearfully back towards Seb but the Doctor was already handling him.

Numbly, Jade allowed the valet to usher her along winding paths towards the Roundhouse. People strolled past; expensively dressed, bejewelled people at leisure, it seemed. Jade's nudity acutely embarrassed her but it aroused little interest or comment among the guests. They, it seemed, were used to seeing naked females under discipline.

Many beautiful young women attended their needs and, although clad, the gorgeous silk gowns revealed as much as they concealed. There were young men there, too, some virtually naked and others adorned with exotic, revealing costumes.

The valet led his charge into the Roundhouse, down a spiral of stone steps and into a spacious cellar. It was pleasantly cool after the searing heat of the midday sun. Low-wattage electric lamps cast long shadows in the basement's gloom. The cellar was a large, cavernous room and Jade quaked as she saw an array of implements adorning one wall: whips, rods, canes...

Two more valets were playing backgammon at a table in the centre of the room. Their strange costumes - red jackets, breeches, stockings and buckled shoes - were totally alien to her, almost as if deriving from another age.

"A new acquisition, in quarantine," the escort said, thrusting Jade forward.

One of the valets sighed and rose from his chair. He flicked a control switch and Jade jumped as bright arc lights immediately illuminated her body. She hung her head as he frankly looked at her nude charms.

Meanwhile, the other valet went to a large box beside the wall. He rummaged inside it and finally produced three strap-like objects, bringing them to where Jade stood. "Raise your head," he ordered, unceremoniously locking a broad leather collar about her throat.

The leather felt stiff and uncomfortable on her neck and its width forced Jade to raise her chin to avoid unpleasant chafing. The man then took her right wrist and affixed a band of softer leather; this he clipped to a ring at

28

the rear of her collar and Jade stood awkwardly as her left wrist was similarly secured. The man cupped her right breast in one hand and drew a mark on the yielding flesh with what she thought was a thick crayon: the broad black marks, just above the nipple, formed the letter Q.

He laughed each time she flinched.

Then, startled, she felt the other man's hand delve between her buttocks and his forefinger press upon the tight rose of her anus. "Up, my beauty," he said, increasing the upward pressure. "Up. More."

Terrified, Jade rose on her toes as the finger threatened penetration. She realised in horror that she had obeyed without question, as if it were her natural role. He held her like that for some seconds before removing his hand. Turned, she could not resist a quick look into the man's face. He immediately cuffed her ear.

"Did they tell you never to look us in the eye?" he asked, taking hold of her shaking shoulders.

Jade dropped her gaze. She saw his hands descend over her heaving breasts and watched a strong thumb trace around the black mark. His other hand teased her left nipple, pinching and rolling the protruding little button until it became hard and pert.

"You must always keep your legs apart," he murmured, as his hand coursed down over her belly. "You are always to remain open."

Jade's body jerked as his rough fingers settled upon her large, protuberant clitoris. The man looked at his colleague in surprise, stepping back but maintaining his hold upon the fleshy nubbin.

"Look what we have here," he said with some pleasure.

Jade froze as the other man stooped to examine her sex, gently parting the fleeced lips. She gave a small startled squeal as the man standing behind suddenly pulled her backwards. Instinctively, Jade parted her legs to regain balance, and the valet held her thus, leaned back, thighs opened, inspected. She closed her eyes to shut out the humiliation.

"I have seen many women," the valet said, "but none with a clit like that."

"Remember she's quarantined," the escort grinned as he released hold of her and turned to leave.

Jade could scarcely believe that this was happening to her. It was almost as if the cameo involved someone else, that she was watching it from afar. The pampered and wealthy Jade Preston was now naked and confined in a dank cellar on a remote island! She was not even allowed to look into the face of her gaolers. It was so hard to resist a constant, instinctive urge to close her thighs tightly. Jade strove to obey their strange rules, not wishing to be beaten again.

They beat her anyway. It was not done in punishment but more routine, almost as if they did not even consider the meaning of the act. The valet attached her wrists to a hook above her head. Jade had not realised what was about to happen and the first lash literally slammed her against the pillar. Her legs wrapped around the unyielding concrete and her eyes opened wide at the astonishing, awful pain.

The second blow caused her to scream. Her anguished writhing caused the scourge to stripe her belly and the front of her thighs, too. After a while, learning quickly, Jade remained pressed tightly against the concrete, hanging by her wrists, with legs and thighs clasped on either side of the broad pillar. Her piteous screams and sobbing pleas were futile. The quaintly-costumed fellow diligently applied the whip until her thighs and rear cheeks glowed with a fiery hue.

When they released her, it was without explanation. She was propelled, stumbling and half-swooning, towards an arched opening at the rear of the cellar. "Run," the valet ordered and she felt the sharp smack of his flat hand across the soreness of her buttocks.

After a moment of shocked hesitation, Jade broke into a stumbling run followed by the chivvying valet.

"Knees up. Higher. Higher."

Each order was accompanied by another sharp, stinging slap. Jade tried to obey but her strength was almost exhausted. She passed barred recess after barred recess. Many of the naked occupants stood gripping the bars, looking on passively as she lurched past, hands confined behind her neck, breasts bouncing rhythmically.

"Halt," the valet commanded, and Jade gratefully stopped before an empty cell and leaned heavily against its bars. "You must not speak or make any other noise."

The valet thrust Jade onto a timber platform in the austere cell and chained her collar to a ring that was set in the wall. He locked the barred gate and wandered off, whistling. Jade, her hands still secured to the collar, began to sob. There was not much to see in her pen: a wooden-backed hairbrush, a large mirror, a covered enamelled pail, presumably for her wastes...

She could hear the clip of stoutly-shod shoes in the tunnel, barred gates opening and shutting, the sound of men's voices and, occasionally, female responses. Jade had heard the sounds of liquid falling into a metal container. Then a valet passed her cell with only a cursory glance. Presently everything was quiet. Suddenly, without warning, the basement was plunged into darkness. It was impossible to see inches in front in the Stygian blackness.

"Hello?" called a whispered male voice. "Don't be frightened. They turn the lights on again in the morning."

"Oh God!" exclaimed Jade, sobs catching her breath.

"Ssh," the other urged. "If they hear us talking, they'll beat us. What day is it?"

"Wednesday. How long have you been here?"

"I don't know. Two weeks, I think. Is it night outside?"

"It's - it's midday."

"Silence!" A loud voice boomed in the blackness and Jade could hear footsteps as someone strode around the perimeter tunnel. A flashlight illuminated her cell and a valet peered through the bars. "Sleep!" he commanded.

Jade, confined as she was, tried to find a sleeping position that would not cause pain.

Two days later, valets hauled Natasha Tranter from a helicopter. They dragged her by the hair, doubled over, her head forced down to waist level. A small rowing boat bobbed gently by the side of the platform. Angrily, the petulant young woman slapped the man's hand away when he released his painful grip.

This was like a nightmare for her. She was still trying to come to terms with the events of the past two days. Sasha, her Russian guide and erstwhile paramour, had not been all he seemed. Once aboard the 'soft-class' of the Trans-Siberian Express, in a private sleeping apartment, he had fucked her vigorously. She was still naked and breathless when a conductor unlocked the apartment door to admit two other men. Natasha's first horrified reaction was that the Russian authorities had, at long last, come to reclaim her.

The rest was a drug-befuddled haze. She vaguely remembered being bundled into an aircraft and when she later regained her senses Natasha found herself strapped in the helicopter, flying high over a deep blue sea. She wore the same short red dress but it was now her only garment: her abductors had obviously hastily pulled it onto her senseless body.

"Come, my lady," the boatman said, holding out his hand.

Natasha stepped awkwardly into the bobbing craft. She sat on the rough plank that served as a seat, closing her knees tightly. The boatman smiled and rowed leisurely to the jetty.

"Where do you take me now?" she demanded as the Head Valet grasped her arm and roughly pulled her ashore.

He slapped Natasha smartly across the face by way of answer. Here she would learn that it did not pay to speak without permission. It was always the same when they first arrived on the island, indignant and still proud.

The next female arrival on the island came voluntarily. The Host's guest was a young raven-haired woman of tawny complexion. The Host himself greeted Serita Fernandez, helping her from the helicopter and leading her across green lawns towards the Roundhouse.

Serita was avidly taking in her new surroundings. Guests sought shade in the gardens from the noon day sun, and some lounged beside a large pool. A couple of delectable bare-breasted creatures lay on the mossy grass with an overweight individual who, although clad only in shorts, proclaimed his wealth with gold adornments.

The gardens were ornamented by bound, helpless creatures. All naked, their bodies contorted and strapped to various devices set at strategic points. A young nude Adonis hung upside down, spread-eagled, tied to a large wheel, and the weight of his massively stiff organ caused it to lie against his navel. A pretty, black haired woman was painfully bent and arched over a large barrel that had been set upon a high cradle; she looked up at the blue sky, eyes closed against the fierce sun, seemingly oblivious to those who viewed her opened private lips displayed amid tight black curls. Another woman sat astride a large statue of a rearing stallion and, as she raised herself slightly to ease her position, Serita saw that the pommel of the marble statue was embedded into the woman's vagina.

"Punishment, my dear," the Host explained as Serita gazed up at the woman. "All of these exhibits are being punished for misdemeanours. It is good for their souls."

Elsewhere, many beautiful women attended the guests. Serita immediately recognised their style of dress: it was similar to that worn by her husband's sluts. The young women wore gaily coloured satin gowns over starched white petticoats. The open neck style of these gowns presented bared breasts raised by a bodice that tightly constricted the waist. Some women served with their skirts hitched up behind to expose naked buttocks, or in front, rolled and carefully tied at the midriff. Serita shot a scornful glance at the Host.

"The style of dress has historical significance," the Host said with a shrug. "Our long-standing patrons would never countenance a change."

"And I will train these slaves?"

"Yes, my dear," he smiled. "That is the notion of it."

"Ah, it will grieve my pig of a husband," Serita replied with satisfaction. "He only reluctantly accepts that I, too, am strong with such women."

The Host looked at her quizzically. "Such women?" he asked.

"Women who need to be helpless at the feet of men."

"In our experience, we can condition any woman or man in that way."

"Not I!" she spat, her eyes flashing.

The Host led her into the cool interior of The Roundhouse. This was the hub of the complex. The place was a hive of activity as people cleaned and prepared for the activities that evening.

"We call it Big Hall," he explained. "Most guests gather here each evening and we provide suitable entertainment. We require all acquisitions to serve here. You may be interested in what lies below."

When they descended into the basement, the two valets there hastily rose to their feet, thong whips swinging from their belts. "Sir?" one asked, moving to grasp Serita by the arm.

"No, you dolt," the Host snapped. "This lady is a new addition to our training staff. Treat her with respect. Where is the latest special acquisition?"

"Number 14, Sir."

The young valet deferentially stepped aside as the Host guided Serita through the arched entrance. She gazed about her in the gloom as they made their way along the narrow tunnel, and saw that each man or woman captive watched with a mixture of curiosity and apprehension.

"We call this the Dungeon," the Host explained in hushed tones. "The imagery suitably impresses our inmates. We hold each new acquisition for a quarantine period here. Of course, this is where their training and conditioning begin."

"You keep your slaves naked?"

"Some have returned to the island for periodic refresher training. We confine others here for punishment or instruction. Ah, here we are."

The Host had stopped at Cell 14, labelled with both a number and a crudely chalked sign: "Natasha". A blonde woman lay unconscious there, legs sprawled across a rough palliasse that served as a bed. Serita saw that a broad leather collar circled the woman's throat. Even in the dim light, Serita could see familiar, angry marks of chastisement that striped the side of the captive's thighs.

"Natasha arrived earlier today," the Host explained. "She must have gone into shock. Sometimes the whip isn't enough to prevent it and we have to use sedatives."

The fair-haired woman suddenly groaned, twisted, and then sank back into restless sleep. For the first time Serita noticed the silence. Only the occasional nervous cough and, sometimes a moan, disturbed the stillness. The Spanish woman peered critically at the sprawled naked figure.

"This woman is not beautiful," she declared after some moments. "Her breasts are uneven, she is too fat, and her nose is crooked. I do not understand."

The Host explained that Natasha Tranter was a very special acquisition, and he admitted that she was perhaps not particularly beautiful. Most of the others were common stock, he said, carefully selected for the supply of particular markets.

"You are right, of course. We prefer that special acquisitions are also attractive in case we have to sell them with the common acquisitions. I shall have to see what can be done to make her beautiful. In this case it is not so important."

Serita did not try to understand his enigmatic words. She merely snorted her contempt for the woman and then wandered around the tunnel. Prisoners blanched under her stare. They seemed humiliated by the frank inspection of a clothed, free woman who was so obviously their superior. This particularly applied to the men with their cocks and balls slung in small leather harnesses. Heads bowed, they sullenly suffered the woman's smiling appraisal.

"This one is pretty," Serita said as she stared at Jade Preston, who stood awkwardly and blushing crimson behind the bars.

"She also is a very special acquisition," the Host said, as if the woman could not hear. "Jade Preston - the wife of an international arms dealer."

34

CHAPTER FOUR

Weeks passed and John Preston heard nothing from his missing wife. After a couple of months, he sadly accepted that Jade would not return.

The British police had been informed. Once satisfied that there was no foul play on Preston's part, they simply recorded the facts without much interest. There was no news media coverage. Life went on. There was business. Suddenly, in fact, there was more business than Preston could comfortably handle. Powerful buyers he had been vainly pursuing for months, years even, suddenly, out of the blue, began to contact him. Thus, he headed for Turkey to organise a deal that was too good to refuse. The trading of arms is a nefarious and chancy business and John Preston was adept at the cloak and dagger preliminaries. Anyway, there was nothing to keep him in England and a stay abroad would be good.

It was all too easy. The deal in Istanbul turned out to be everything that had been promised, although it took some weeks to arrange. The sensual delights of Turkey took him by surprise, though. Flying in on a very clear day - the wonderful panorama of the wide Bosphorous and the Golden Horn provided a magical moment - he was greeted at the airport by a smartly-uniformed and stunningly attractive chauffeuse. The girl, a young Armenian, introduced herself as Leila and added that she had been placed completely at his disposal. Preston noted her strong emphasis on the word 'completely'.

Leila insisted on submissively addressing him as "sir" with almost every sentence. The beautiful girl meaningfully rippled the fingers of her left hand, pointedly showing the iron ring upon her third finger. It meant nothing to Preston. On arrival at the villa, Leila introduced Rachel, the housekeeper. Preston could not quite believe his eyes; Rachel, a dark haired, sloe-eyed Jewish woman, was as breathtakingly beautiful as the chauffeuse and, moreover, she displayed her charms in a semi-diaphanous caftan that wafted alluringly in the cooling breeze to give tantalising glimpses of the promise beneath. Preston ate the meal which awaited him, his suave manner slightly undone by the eager and deferential attentiveness of the women.

"Master!" Leila called.

Preston glanced up from his meal, beginning, "Look, I-"

His words were stifled in surprise. Leila, completely naked, posed seductively, her eyes carefully downcast. Preston stared wide-eyed at the vision: perfect breasts, trim waist, flaring hips.

"Are you not pleased with your girl?" Leila asked.

Pleased! Preston was enthralled and excited by the erotic adornments on her magnificent body: both of Leila's pert, dark nipples were pierced with gleaming, golden rings.

"She is sometimes chained by those rings," Rachel explained.

"We are your servants, Sir," Leila added. "Your servants in all things. We expect strict discipline and would not wish you to submit a bad report."

Rachel took a short-handled, multi-lash whip from a hook on the wall. She approached Harcourt, sank to her knees, and offered the implement to him. "You must beat us if you are displeased."

"Get up!" Preston snapped, hurling aside the whip.

Rachel sprang to her feet and immediately adopted a submissive pose. "May I speak?" she asked. "We are your women. More than that, we must teach you how to be a strong master. Those are our instructions."

Leila smiled and added, "You will not be disappointed. Both Rachel and myself have been trained by experts."

After only one week of luxurious and sensuous living at the villa in Istanbul, a message arrived for John Preston. Someone was travelling from London to see him. A policeman! Wariness was a tool of John Preston's trade. Jade used to tease that he was paranoid. However, John's innate sense of danger had often served him well. Never at ease with the civil police in any country, Preston imagined smelling the unpleasant aroma of the burning flesh of a sacrificial lamb.

His suspicions were confirmed when the man arrived at the villa. He was tall and well into middle-age, wearing a white Panama hat. He simply announced himself as the Policeman, offering no other name, and Preston knew better than to press him further. Dismissing Rachel, whose state of undress seemed to have been unnoticed by the visitor, Preston took the man into the enclosed courtyard where they sat in the shade of a palisaded verandah.

"It is safe to talk here," he said.

"You have contacts throughout the world, Mr Preston," the Policeman began, glancing warily round the courtyard, "particularly the Balkans. And you are adept at entering and leaving countries without arousing too much attention. Serbia and Iraq, for example..."

Preston's handsome features creased in a frown. This man knew too much. The British Foreign Office fellows had obviously been talking. He smiled grimly. "You seem to have wasted your journey here. I really think you have the wrong man."

"My interest is entirely unconnected with the arms trade," the Policeman said, as if in reassurance, but causing Preston to start inwardly.

"Then why are you here? It's a long way from London."

The Policeman eased back and removed his white Panama hat. "Let me tell you a story," he said. "Some years ago a secret society maintained an estate in France - a bizarre brothel, in truth. The women there seemed to revel in their degradation. Then there was something of a scandal involving murder and they disbanded the French society. No charges were laid - you know the French in these things."

"Where is this leading?"

"Then a devious operator known only as The Host set up an outfit that he simply calls 'the organisation' - doesn't even spell it with a capital 'O'. This organisation simply snatches and enslaves young men and women."

"Sorry," Preston said, rising from his chair. "Not my sort of thing, I'm afraid."

The Policeman waved away Preston's interruption and continued in his broad, Northern accent.

"The organisation is nothing more than a gang of white slavers. According to my information, they drug and transport their victims to a privately-owned Greek island where the man who calls himself The Host has recreated the services of the old French society. His victims are held there for anything up to a year before being sold to selected buyers."

"All very interesting, but..."

"The organisation also kidnaps the wives of wealthy men for ransom. Reports mention figures of half a million pounds or more."

Preston sighed. The Policeman was obviously not going to leave until he had had his say. So, sitting and lighting another small cigar, he patiently listened as the man went on to tell of the worldwide network of brothels and vice rackets. At bottom, the Policeman said, it was nothing more nor less than old-fashioned white-slavery.

Preston raised his eyebrows when the man named many rich, powerful and very high-profile figures: alleged associates and customers of the vice ring. It was an incredible story of wealthy masters and bonded slaves

"My chaps nearly had this nab, the Host, a few weeks ago in one of the organisation's clip-joints in London... the Bond-Age Club?" - the Policeman paused and waited for a response but Preston was too controlled a man for that - "You were there that night, of course."

"Really?"

"I couldn't arrest the Host in Britain... no real evidence... merely intended to have a word with him. One of my chaps badly bungled it. The damned fool actually fired a pistol shot. But then, you know that - you intervened."

"Forgive my cynicism," Preston said, "but I smell a setup here. Someone mysteriously invited me to the Bond-Age Club that night."

The Policeman ignored Preston's interjection. "The Host thinks that was the work of an American hoodlum by the name of Tranter. He is unaware of my interest. I have a reliable informant: she is a woman who originally served the old society and who now manages the Bond-Age Club. Unfortunately, this woman does not know the location of the island, although they have often taken her there. That is where you come in."

"This is completely out of my line."

"They have your wife..."

"WHAT?"

"It is true. They have your wife. And, er, a young fellow by the name of Sebastian Moore."

Preston had recovered from the shock quickly: he was a cool customer, the Policeman saw. But now raised eyebrows momentarily betrayed surprise. "How would you know that?"

"As I said, I have an excellent source."

"If it is true," Preston conceded, "it may change my attitude. There is one thing that bothers me: you speak as if this were a personal matter."

"Ah," the Policeman said, rising to his feet, "you are very perceptive, Mr Preston. I do have a very special interest in that island."

CHAPTER FIVE

Jade Preston's first days on that island were mundane. Exercised each morning, showered, and then long hours chained in her cell.

Valets invariably attached her wrists to the collar about her neck. It was a strange feeling being unable to touch her own sex, to soothe the yearnings these people had aroused there. She was in quarantine, awaiting the Doctor's clearance. Although the punishments were harsh, there was always the strange reassurance that they would never truly damage her. It was a strict code, she was told. Their whips might bite ferociously, even raising huge welts, but her skin was never broken. Somehow, despite the abuse, she was safe.

Besides herself and Sebastian, another woman had only recently arrived in the Dungeon; Jade watched them run the blonde past her cell and saw that the valets were especially cruel to her. The rules did not allow the slaves talk but the would sometimes manage whispered conversations.

Jade learned that the woman was another 'special acquisition': reputedly a famous Russian gymnast and the wife of a notorious American gangster. The special acquisitions received no concessions and the valets treated them at least as badly as they did the rest. And, like the others, they were quarantined and unavailable for full sexual usage.

Yet still the organisation made some use of the new slaves: a dozen now, eight women and four men. One evening they took Jade to one of the many side-rooms in the Dungeon. The room came as a pleasant surprise to her: it was bright, clean, and furnished with mirrors and grooming tables. Most of the other new slaves were already there, including the special acquisitions. The valet ordered Jade to hands and knees upon one of the padded tables. She saw her reflection in one of the many mirrors and drew some secret pride that her breasts depended so beautifully.

"Oh!" she exclaimed in shock as her anus was peremptorily penetrated and, almost immediately, she felt a warm liquid gurgling within her. The humiliation! She could not protest and merely hung her head between stiff arms as her belly seemed to swell.

"Hold that until given permission to release it," a valet ordered. and she felt the cool rim of a bowl touching the insides of her thighs. "Now!"

Jade gratefully relaxed and felt the liquid gush into the bowl.

"Shower and douche," the man ordered.

She leapt from the table and scurried to the showers, past where Sebastian knelt as he received the same internal cleansing. After a hot shower the douche was icy cold within Jade's vagina and it seemed to constrict the secret flesh there. She liked that. Then like the others, she returned and lay compliantly under the sensual hands of a skilled masseuse.

The woman kneaded Jade's flesh, probing into every cranny of her body, between the buttocks, into the hairline at the base of her neck, thighs, ankles, even the soles of her feet. Only when ordered to her back did Sally see that the woman was applying a silvery lotion, rubbing the lustrous pigment into the skin beneath her fingers, every inch of it. Even the tight pubic curls were combed through with the substance. Jade lay there, not knowing what else to do. There was something highly sensuous in being so adorned.

The other slaves were receiving similar treatment, even Angelique, a black French woman; Jade saw that the silver coating was much deeper hued on the ebony base, and she could not help but be fascinated as Angelique docilely allowed the masseur to rub silver oil into one of her large breasts. She lay there with legs splayed and Jade could see the moist sex between the woman's dark sex lips, vividly pink.

And the male slaves. They seemed particularly and strangely enhanced by the shining silver that so well displayed their rippling muscles. The men's cocks, deliberately teased to full erection, were also painted, adding emphasis to the gleaming heads.

All of the slaves' lips, and their eyelids too, were painted with a shiny metallic lacquer. Then their nipples were similarly painted, and Jade nearly swooned as the fine brush tickled her sensitised flesh; the valet who performed this task appeared not to notice. Finally, their hair was concealed under silver wigs - Jade's was long and flowing. The result was surreal: each slave positively glowed from head to toe with a bright silver that shone beneath the strong lights.

"Line up. You will walk well," they were warned. 'Well' meant as sexily as possible, very upright and with a provocative swing to the body.

Standing immediately behind Sally Clark, Jade's eyes fixed upon her swaying silver buttocks as they filed from the Dungeon. A true slave, this one, Jade thought as Sally straightened consciously, proudly, when the column emerged into open air.

It was dusk and there were surprisingly few guests about in the gardens. Still, Sally walked well for those who watched, with her stomach taut, breasts thrust forward and eyes cast down.

The men strode forward on the pads of bare feet, muscles and sinews tensed, stiff cocks jutting and bobbing with each step. Jade merely walked, without any attempt for erotic effect. The valets would surely not wish to mar her silver skin that had been so laboriously prepared? This notion was dispelled by a sharp rap of a cane across the crease of her thighs and she hastily adopted Sally's excellent example, unashamedly sashaying along like a beauty queen on parade.

As they crossed the gardens, Jade saw that valets were releasing naked penitents from punishment displays. She shuddered. What these people could do to her!

They went to the Roundhouse, across the plush foyer and into Big Hall. Jade's heart almost stopped. Guests were assembled for their evening entertainment, dining and engaged in idle chatter. When the column entered, walking well, the buzz of conversation seemed to die momentarily. All eyes were upon the silvered slaves as a valet led the line around the perimeter of the large circular floor.

Jade's heart beat madly as she swayed along, her breasts bouncing with each long step. Yet within her belly there was the familiar disquieting warmth borne of delicious exhilaration and excitement. Perhaps it was the silver wig, the paint, almost like a disguise... somehow it did not seem as if Jade Preston was being paraded there, it was someone else, an anonymous and lovely female, and she could enjoy that person's debasement. It was a scene that exceeded her wildest fantasies.

"Halt."

The line stopped dutifully beside one of the many pillars that supported the roof. Jade saw that a placard was affixed to the masonry: 'Angelique'. Beside it was a large statue of a hideously grinning satyr: half man with a pointed beard and protruding pointed tongue, and half goat with a huge erect phallus jutting from its loins. The satyr's large hands were held high at its bearded chin with palms facing upwards, its fingers splayed before his face and thumbs pointing to the roof.

The French girl, Angelique, she who had been black, was summoned forward. Jade watched, fascinated, as Angelique obediently climbed the portable steps set beside the pillar. She did not question their intent, not even with an enquiring glance. Jade looked up and saw that the wide, smoothly polished pillar was decorated on either side with ornate filials some six feet from the ground. Long, strong chains dangled from metal rings set in high the masonry.

Angelique gingerly stepped first onto the satyr's shoulders, clearly concentrating upon the valet's instructions. Then she placed her small feet onto the narrow ledges of the filials so that she was facing the pillar, her legs splayed around it.

Then, as one valet held her, she obediently seized the chains dangling there. She was made to lean back and squat with bent knees, supporting herself by hanging onto the chains. Jade gasped. Angelique's buttocks and gaping pink sex were provocatively displayed. But that was not all. Two valets grunted as they struggled to move the heavy statue; inching it forward, they positioned the hideous figure so that its hands were directly beneath the woman's jutting buttocks.

41

"Down!" the valet commanded.

Angelique obeyed, but she jerked herself up as the cold stone touched her flesh. A lash across her back brought obedience and the black girl slowly lowered her bottom onto the inviting stone hands that formed a perfect saddle for her rounded cheeks. The satyr's upraised thumbs had their purpose: as the woman lowered herself, these digits penetrated and widely spread her vagina and, completing the picture, the poking tongue of the statue seemed to be licking at the her anus. Jade shuddered. There was a burst of applause from the guests as the portable steps were withdrawn. Angelique hung there, displayed, a silvered cameo of ravishment.

"Forward."

At the next station, Sebastian was taken to be confronted by another fiend-ishly grinning satyr. Jade gasped in sympathy and dismay as the valet turned him and backed his silver buttocks against the statue's large, projecting phallus. Sebastian was bent double, stooped beneath a stone arm that seemed to be pressing his neck downwards. Then the valets lifted the captive's hips and carefully lowered him onto the massive penis. Sebastian, looking down, opened his mouth as if to cry out when they impaled him. His eyes first opened wide and then grimaced tightly shut. They left him strapped in posi-tion. He could raise himself on tiptoes, slightly easing the stretch upon his sphincter that was so visible from below, but nothing more. The valets de-scended the steps and, again, there was a ripple of applause for the tableau.

"Forward."

The placard attached to the next pillar bore the legend 'Leah'. One of the two American women stepped forward and, despite the scenes she had just witnessed, she calmly climbed up beside the stone satyr placed there. This hideous statue squatted, contemplating its impossibly rampant cock. In the Dungeon, slaves had whispered that Leah had been a part-time whore in the States. The valet allowed her to grease the satyr's massive organ, and Jade's heart beat more rapidly as she watched Leah's slim hands working up and down the thick shaft. Then the valets took hold of Leah's arms. When they had finished with her, she was impaled astride the monstrous organ, sup-ported by her stiff forearms, hands resting upon the stone beast's wide shoul-ders. Two very short leashes were attached to tight little clamps upon her nipples and fixed to the satyr's outstretched cupped hands, strictly limiting her upward movement.

Jade saw poor Leah trying to raise herself from the unyielding cock. When her soft silver breasts became intolerably distended by the leashes, she slowly lowered down again, impaling herself to the hilt. Leah's large breasts then overflowed from the satyr's cupped hands.

"Forward."

Another of the men was exhibited at the next pillar. He earned a fierce whipping by struggling desperately as the valets impaled his anus upon the penis of another stone satyr. His struggles and his subsequent punishment seemed to heighten the guests' enjoyment. Jade resolved not to give them that pleasure, at least.

"Forward."

Sally now headed the column. She maintained an elegant posture but Jade could hear her quickened breathing. Sally obediently stepped forward and looked anxiously up at the site they had prepared for her. The stone satyr there was standing with its belly protuberant and thick cock thrusting forward; one of its arms was bent at chest height with the palm of its hand upraised, while the other hand was cupped about a foot away from its organ. Sally climbed the steps accompanied by a valet. She took the lubricant and massaged oil onto the length of the penis, using both hands. Jade thought that she could smell the aroma of female arousal and she realised uncomfortably that it could well have come from her own body. With bated breath, she watched the valet manoeuvre Sally into position.

Sally faced the hideous statue, her hand clinging to its neck. She was made to place her left leg high, her thigh resting on the outstretched hand. When the valet lifted Sally to lower her upon the thrusting organ, her buttocks lay in the palm of the monster's other hand. Jade heard the moan as the greased cock stretched Sally's sex. Then they were removing the steps, leaving her there, impaled, with one leg hoisted at the height of her trembling breasts. Then Sally grunted loudly, a sound of surprise, Jade thought, and the valet chuckled.

"Forward."

Almost as if in a trance, Jade walked prettily to the next pillar. 'Jade' the placard announced. She looked up at the statue that awaited her feminine flesh. This one was almost bent double, leaning backwards, supporting itself on one arm. It seemed bigger, its cock larger, than had the others.

Jade's belly fluttered as she walked up the wide steps, feeling the ridged rubber beneath her bare feet. At the top platform she looked across at the huge phallus. The valet took her hand and placed a large glob of lubricating jelly into the palm. She swallowed hard and leaned over to caress the length of the organ. To her surprise, the veined penis was not made of stone like the rest of the statue, but of a slightly yielding rubberised substance. It was wider at the base and her hand could barely encircle it there, but somewhat thinner at the top, although there was a large rounded head to it. She desperately massaged the jelly along its length.

"Enough," the valet said quietly. "Climb."

Jade cast a frightened glance downwards, momentarily frozen with panic.
"Climb!"

He gently lifted her left leg and pulled it across the awful statue, so that she was facing away from its fiendish face. Then the valet's strong arms lifted her and lowered her upon the slickly oiled cock. Jade spread her legs

43

widely, holding her breath. Then it was inside her vagina, all the way, the thickness of the shaft's base almost splitting her. She gasped. Then the man held Jade's left nipple, which was already very erect, and quickly snapped a small silver clamp upon it. He attached the clamp to a hook embedded in the palm of the statue's hand. This produced the effect that the satyr was clutching Jade's left breast. She had never before worn a nipple clamp but it was not as painful as she had imagined, although the small device immediately caused a throbbing sensation; its grip tightened when she pulled against it.

Jade leaned forward, her hands upon the knees of the statue. Using all the strength of her arms, she pushed herself up on the length of the penis as far as she could, reducing the pressure of its wide base. Then, she gave a small squeal as the organ within her began to vibrate, sending a startling tingle through her loins. The vibrations increased with each movement. Strands from the silver wig hung before her eyes as she squirmed upon the stone satyr. Jade heard the guests applauding and she knew that they could clearly see the cock entering her ripe vagina. But did they know that it was pulsing though her very soul?

The steps were drawn away and Jade heard the valet order, "Forward." She was left there, an exhibit for the evening, an erotic decoration. This is how the organisation advertises its future offerings, she thought bitterly. Once out of quarantine, then any one of the guests who now chatted below could have the use of her.

The vibrating cock was indefatigable. Jade lost count of the number of orgasms that she endured that night. They took her down in the small hours, her body throbbing from head to toe.

The weary slaves trudged back to the Dungeon. Each of them seemed to have taken the experience in a different way. Sebastian sobbed quietly. Jade was strangely elated, even though sore and tired. Sally seemed curiously alive, and she walked as well as before, swaying her hips.

CHAPTER SIX

Newly-released from the Dungeon, Sally knelt in silence in the training room, gazing intently at her image reflected in the mirrors. Stark naked, under the eyes of free men. But she was absurdly embarrassed when a beautiful clothed woman entered the room.

Serita was haughty and looked down at the slaves - they who were nude, kneeling with widely spaced thighs - as if they were inferior creatures. She nodded, surveying the images of her own elegantly-attired and trim body, revealed from various angles by the room's strategically-angled mirrors. Sally kept her eyes upon the mirror as she must. The woman paced arrogantly among the slaves.

"It is perhaps good that the sluts constantly see themselves naked," she said. "The men, too."

Sally winced inwardly but remained immobile, staring steadfastly at her own reflection. After the rigours and oppression of the dungeon she had been dreading the training room. However, to her surprise, the valets had made the slaves, male and female, do nothing more than study their naked bodies these first few days. That, and repeat affirmations designed to change their thoughts.

Boredom would have been a major factor had it not been for the trainers' canes and straps: any sign of failing concentration brought swift, painful and humiliating punishment.

So, freshly collared with a loose green-enamelled metal band, much better than the stiff leather, Sally was forced for the first time to gaze at her own intimate curves, not fleetingly before dressing or after bathing, but for hours at a time. And she was somewhat surprised by what she saw: a beautiful, lithe creature with proud, firm breasts and immodestly exposed feminine flesh.

The other women fascinated her too. Often, when sunbathing on foreign beaches, like all women she supposed, Sally had cast furtive glances at the exposed female bodies, gauging her own body against theirs. Now she could frankly measure her naked charms against those of the women so openly displayed around her - indeed, it was a requirement.

And the men, magnificent but submissive, were also objects of her curiosity. She felt curiously liberated to be able to gaze upon their nudity. How subtly different human bodies are, she thought, and this particularly applied to the men with their cocks often straining, tips glistening with moisture.

"Think of when you were a child, three years old," the trainer intoned. "You enjoyed being submissive then, being told what to do. If you disobeyed you were punished. Picture that child. Loved. Safe. You are that child."

Sally gazed at the mirror and tried to use her mind as he bid. It was not easy, for there were many other thoughts. All of the slaves bore the marks of the valets' whips. Faint, thin, blue lines remained across Sally's thighs: whips and, sometimes, a riding crop, cruelly and mercilessly applied. She was flogged every day in the Dungeon, often more than once. Sometimes guests would enter her cell, carrying variously styled whips and scourges or, more painful still, whippy canes. Like every other slave she had come to expect visits, if not from guests then from the seemingly unfeeling valets in their curious uniforms. Usually chained, wrists confined, her eyes lowered, never daring to look at their faces.

"Affirm your right to be a slave. Repeat after me, 'I love and accept myself in my slavery.'"

"I love and accept myself in my slavery. I love and accept myself in my slavery."

"Hold your gaze in the mirror. Say, 'I am free to release my deep sexual needs without inhibition.'"

"I am free to release my deep sexual needs without inhibition."

Sally tried to obey the rules. Her sex was always open to their gaze and, frequently, their hands. Yet she was still beaten. And, more often than not, before or after a beating, she was required to perform oral service; it was the same for all of the women. Did they feel the same way, she wondered? Was the harsh discipline and the punishment having the same effect upon them? It bewildered and worried Sally that her body so freely betrayed her mind. Instantly wet, a warm glow suffusing her stomach, she had begun to gain a strange, forbidden excitement from it all!

There had been a yearning that men - valets, guests, anyone - use her fully and mercilessly.

Now, suddenly, she was free from the Dungeon and her breast no longer bore a quarantine mark. The Host had been the first to take her, as was his privilege. She served him blindfolded, hearing nothing, only feeling, her head encased in a strange mask. After that the valets had been quick to take advantage, regularly commanding her to her back. Some wealthy guests, too, pleasured her until she screamed not for mercy but for more. And when they brought her to a climax, it was all engulfing, obliterating all senses but pain and pleasure. Sally Clark found herself blushing, from face to breasts, as she gazed in the mirror and thought of these things.

"Think of your deepest inhibition," the trainer was saying. "Think - what makes you resist loving yourself as a slave?"

Sally immediately, involuntarily almost, thought of the guilt and shame. What would her friends think, seeing her naked and abused? What would they think if they saw that she willingly participated in her slavery?

"Keep the thought in mind and say, 'I release you'."

"I release you. I release you." Sally said it with feeling, and it was easy, for her friends were not there to see.

"What is your purpose?" the trainer suddenly asked in a loud voice.

Unthinkingly, the slaves replied: "To serve."

"How do you serve?"

"With instant obedience," they cried. "I love and accept myself in my slavery."

Serita suddenly laughed and tears of humiliation filled Sally's eyes. The valets and trainers were conditioning her like an animal. Seemingly ridiculous responses had been drilled into them all under the threat of punishment and, after only a few days, their reaction to familiar questions was becoming automatic. They were being relentlessly prepared for subservience.

Initially unconcerned by this crude psychology and quite certain that it would not affect her, Sally had obediently mouthed the required phrases to avoid punishment. It was a childish game. Suddenly, however, perhaps because of Serita's contemptuous laugh, she realised that the mind-games were beginning to work. Sally Clark really was beginning to love and accept herself in her slavery.

"Change position," the trainer called. "Pose."

Pose, indeed! But, like the others, men and women, Sally immediately rose to her feet and adopted a seductive stance. It was no longer necessary to remind her to keep her legs apart. Gazing ahead at the image, she could see her pert rear reflected in the mirror behind her. Sally also saw four male guests quietly enter the room. They stood and gazed appreciatively at the nude trainees. It was a frequent occurrence: guests often visited to watch trainers putting new slaves through their paces. Sometimes women came, too, and Sally imagined that, as these superior beings watched her humiliation, they were secretly wondering what it would be like if they too were helplessly enslaved. But, still, Sally was always utterly embarrassed by their presence.

"I love and accept myself in my slavery," she wordlessly reminded herself.

"Good afternoon." The Host cordially greeted the onlookers as he guided Serita from the room. When outside, he told her: "We encourage guests to observe training sessions. It makes the acquisitions try harder."

"Animals!" Serita said with a sneer. "What will you do with them when they are trained?"

The Host explained that the slaves would be sold to clients for private and complete servitude, for high class brothels or as exclusive but utterly compliant playthings.

The organisation was not overly concerned with the ultimate usage of their captives. Until their sale, they would serve guests who visited the island, fully and submissively. All would be relentlessly trained in the erotic arts. There was a constant retrading of such chattels. Some returned to the island a number of times. Later, perhaps wearing a distinctive iron ring upon the third finger of the left hand, they would reappear, experienced and docile, in vice dens like the Bond- Age Club in London.

What happens to an ageing white slave? Lily had been relatively lucky: the all-powerful organisation had assigned her to manage the Bond-Age Club. Lily knew that she was directly accountable for the activities and profits of the enterprise. Failure would be an unpleasant experience.

She leaned on the bar and surveyed the basement room of the Club. An ordinary night, much like any other: businessmen indulging in a pale recreation of erotic fantasies before commuting to their respectable, boring wives. Lily looked critically at the young men and women who paraded there in their chains and harnesses.

The Bond-Age was distinguished by the quality of its staff. The women sent to Lily always had a certain class. And the men, too, with their oiled muscles. They were frequently replaced and none stayed there long enough to become stale. Sometimes they came fresh from the island but, more often than not, they were experienced hands and utterly subservient by the time they reached Lily.

She was a strict mistress and ruled her charges with a firm hand, for, ultimately, she must answer to the organisation. Anyway, the ordeal of those under her command was no harsher than she herself had experienced. The madam, for that is what she had become, was almost forty years old now. Yet customers continued to demand her services and, when so required, she had to perform as abjectly and totally as her girls. Lily, like the young men and women she controlled, was available for the profit of the organisation. That was how it was and how it had been for over twenty years.

The Policeman had become a regular visitor. Lily disliked him almost as much as she feared the Host, but the man seemed to represent her only hope of escape. Yes, after all those years, Lily still hoped for escape, not just from the club - that would be easy - but from the long reach of the organisation.

That night she scarcely spoke to the Policeman. He was sitting alone on a tall stool beside the bar when five or six men burst into the bar, brutally smashing aside the guard hired by the Club. They wielded iron bars and sledgehammers. Amid terrified screams of women and the panic of scuttling patrons, the hoodlums proceeded to wreck the place. The Policeman, calmly downed the remains of his drink before wandering to the exit.

Lily stood as if mesmerised amid the mayhem, watching the systematic destruction. Tables, chairs, bar fittings, liquor bottles... little was left in one piece.

When they had finished one man approached Lily. He grasped the hem of her dress and roughly hoisted it up. She stood transfixed as he thrust a small business card into the top of her black stocking. Then, without a word, they left. Lily retrieved the card and read aloud: 'Felix Tranter Enterprises'. She quaked. The Host would not be pleased. Lily was afraid, and she immediately decided to contact others, the shadowy people who ruled the Host himself.

A mistake!

Lily, accompanied by three hard-faced men, arrived at the island less than twenty-four hours later. They immediately went to the second floor of the Roundhouse, to the Host's private office.

"The Host has left strict orders not to be disturbed," the secretary said.

Her orders mattered little, however, for the three men simply strode past, dragging Lily behind them. They entered the Host's inner sanctum and the two burly valets who stood guard immediately stepped aside to allow entry into his office. The Host was busying himself with a woman who was stretched on the cool marble floor clad in nothing but his feathered mask.

"I'm sorry, sir, they just walked past me," the secretary said, hurrying after the men in dismay.

"Get your women out of here - we have confidential business."

Although the secretary immediately withdrew, the masked nude remained prone upon the floor, her legs splayed. "You are perfectly safe," said the Host, adjusting his clothing. "She can neither see nor hear behind the mask."

"We want to know what the hell is going on," one of the men declared. "Tranter's boys have wrecked the Bond-Age. This bitch" - the man paused to thrust forward the trembling Lily - "was our manager, right? She tells us that you knew about an attempted takeover by Felix Tranter."

"Quite so."

"Quite so?" one of the men growled, leaning forward to grasp the fabric of the Host's shirt. "Then why is this clown still walking? More to the point, why is he free to wreck one of our properties?"

Showing obvious distaste, the Host calmly removed the man's hand from his shirt and fastidiously smoothed the crumpled silk. He stepped over the nude woman and coolly walked to sit behind his polished desk. "It is all in hand," he said.

"Shit! We can replace you if necessary."

"This is my organisation," the Host said, his eyes narrowing. "I have consistently brought you excellent profits. Leave Tranter to me." Then, suddenly smiling, he added, "While you are here, do feel free to enjoy yourselves."

After some hesitation, the three men left the office. Lily remained, standing before the Host, who pressed a bell-push as he stared at her.

"I thought you were my creature, Lily," he said, "and yet you divulge highly confidential and sensitive information to others. Why did you inform my associates of this trouble rather than myself?"

"They must have discovered it from someone else," she stammered.

The Host raised disbelieving eyebrows. "You have not pleased me, Lily."

A young valet appeared at the door, summoned by the bell. The Host stepped around his desk and approached Lily. She trembled as he moved towards her. "Did I buy this dress for you?" he asked, fingering the material.

"You have provided everything I own."

"You own nothing then," he said, positioning a high-backed, wooden chair at the centre of the room. "I want it all back, Lily. You must be punished. You know the procedure."

Lily clearly knew what must follow. Slowly, she removed her elegant dress. Then she kicked off her shoes, unfastened the half-brassiere that invitingly lifted her otherwise bared breasts, stripped off the narrow corset that constricted her waist, and removed her stockings. Standing naked before the Host, Lily instinctively thrust out her breasts and sucked in her belly; it was an act born of years of conditioning. Without receiving another word of command, inhaling deeply, she leaned over the back of the chair, her hands grasping the edges of its wooden seat. Lily took some care and time in arranging her position: rising high on the tips of her toes, taut legs together, her bottom upraised and presented for punishment. The Host returned to his seat behind the desk and nodded to the valet.

The first blow of the valet's cane made Lily leap convulsively. She gasped and her eyes widened. Then, breathing deeply, she struggled to regain her composure. In the seemingly long seconds which followed, she resumed her position, rising high on her toes again. As she awaited the next searing stripe, her buttocks tightened.

"Relax," the valet ordered. "More."

His fingers gently stroked the soft cheeks. The next four strokes each made her screech and her reddened buttocks seemed to dance under the cane. Then, without a word of command, Lily, slowly, painfully, altered her position. She turned the chair and leaned over once more, this time with legs widely splayed, her glowing rear facing the Host. Her sex was openly and widely displayed. Again the searing cane bit into her flesh. The masked nude stirred slightly on the floor, unaware of the happenings around her.

They took their leisure in punishing Lily. Eventually she was reduced to a sobbing and begging animal.

"Strict punishment regime," the Host ordered for Lily, before roughly using the masked woman. "Take her to the Dungeon."

CHAPTER SEVEN

Jade looked up with mild interest to see the naked woman high-stepping past her cell. It was a common occurrence in the Dungeon, although the woman seemed older than the others. The humiliating prancing run that made a woman's breasts ache was all part of the scheme to break her spirit. Shortly afterwards, the Dungeon was plunged into blackness and Jade, her hands already confined, settled to sleep.

She lay in the blackness pondering her slavery and, more importantly, her reaction to it. She knew that the system was beginning to break down her own resistance. Her body was becoming conditioned by the routine. So, when the meal bell sounded, Jade found herself salivating and hungry. And, when given permission to break the deathly silence in the Dungeon, she, like everyone else, eagerly shouted questions to the others, screamed and, once, even sang loudly.

When the order for silence came, an immediate hush always fell upon the basement again.

And, each morning, when valets released the captives from their chains, Jade obediently presented her naked body for inspection. Waiting at the bars of her cell, she stood with hands on head, legs widely spaced and tongue out in the prescribed manner. A valet would carefully place a contraceptive pill on her tongue and wait until it was swallowed.

After this, when the barred gate was opened, she would unhesitatingly step into the tunnel and, standing in a line of other nude slaves, await the signal. When the whistle blew, she would obediently run around the circular tunnel, completing lap after lap until breathless and perspiring freely. Pace and style was dictated by a trainer who ran with them, constantly varying his speed and the action required. The concern of each inmate was to keep a required distance from the prisoner immediately in front and to copy his or her changes of style, sometimes sprinting madly; sometimes leaping to touch the arched roof of the tunnel as they ran. Valets stood at strategic points to punish the tardy with their stinging whips.

Jade no longer gave much thought to the narcissistic Sebastian. He seemingly revelled in his degradation and positively enjoyed the physical workouts that were honing the outline of his already finely sculpted body to perfection.

After the exercise each day, the valets required the slaves, men and women together, to squat on Turkish toilets. Jade hated this humiliating imposition but it happened each morning and evening. Then there would be the luxury of a shower. The valets were ever watchful that their male and female prisoners did not dally intimately with each other. However, in the press of slick flesh in the shower room, Jade often felt her soft breasts or buttocks being illicitly fondled, or an erect penis nudging against her. On one occasion, she had stood transfixed as the fingers of a male slave slipped into her sex lips; Jade had blushed hotly and turned away but she made no complaint. It was perhaps natural, for these were young, healthy people kept in erotic captivity, their sexual urges largely unsatisfied.

Upon returning to her cell, Jade would brush her hair and then - nothing. There was nothing else to do but sit in silence for the remainder of the day and await the visits of valets and guests. When would they come? Would they come? It was a senseless rhetorical question, for each day someone would come. Chains and cuffs, confinement to the sleeping platform, whips and pain, lips required for service. Yes, someone would come. Jade knew that she would submit to the ordeal without protest.

Until then she could read the explicit pornographic book which was always available in the cell. Or she could study the reflection of her naked body in the full-length mirror there. Boredom was a major conditioning tool. The 'noisy hour' was so eagerly anticipated. Meals, though tasteless, became a highlight of the day. Visits and the attendant beatings and degradation were both dreaded and anticipated. After some time in the Dungeon, in fact, Jade even began to welcome the visits of guests.

Jade found it horribly degrading to present herself before demanding visitors. These aloof powerful people, clothed and infinitely superior, would stroll to her cell and gaze through the bars at her nude body. It was an ordeal and she must not look directly into their faces, nor could she close her thighs. And, sometimes, they would require her to pose.

At first she had been horrified and refused to comply but the beating which followed merely presented the guests with added titillation. After that, like most of the others, she had striven to please. When the guests had moved on, Jade invariably wept, full of self-hatred at her abject submission, though she was secretly thrilled by it.

Usually, the visitors were male. They enjoyed giving precise instructions, making her contort her nude body this way and that. It had been infinitely worse when a young raven-haired woman clad in expensive designer casuals had visited the dungeon - a haughty creature with an imperious air. Jade had been whipped for daring to gaze at the exquisite but cruel features. This woman mercilessly put Jade through a series of degrading poses that displayed every crevice of her body.

"Stoop on one knee, hands in your hair, look angry," the woman had ordered. "On your back, knees flexed and apart. Stretch out your left leg, toes pointed... now roll over, stomach high, thrust back your buttocks... no, girl.

Again!"

Jade quickly learned the importance of pleasing the Spanish woman. On many subsequent visits this visitor ordered that inmates be whipped, and the valets duly complied. The cruel beauty required that Jade thank her after each beating. Serita returned many times and seemed to relish the opportunity of humiliating the hapless Jade in particular.

Jade thought about all of these things as she lay in the unnatural blackness. A valet's torch suddenly illuminated her cell. He released the chain about her collar and ordered, "Stand up, if you please. Stand on the platform."

Jade scrambled to her feet. The valets were unbelievably cruel. They appeared to have the right to beat her whenever they wished. No reason or infraction of rules was required. They merely came into the cell and thrashed her. Jade knew that it happened to the others as well, and the men among them wept and pleaded for mercy no less than the women. She also knew that many other slaves were frequently required to satisfy the lusts of the valets. Often in the night there were the sounds of men and women in the throes of submission, astonishingly often pleading for more. None of the valets ever attempted to use Jade's body fully. Yet, with increasing frequency, she was obliged to pleasure them with her mouth.

"On your toes," the valet commanded civilly, standing on the platform beside Jade. "Higher."

He chained her wrists above her head and pulled the chain taut, painfully stretching her arms. The shortened chain left her standing, strained, on tiptoes.

The valet stepped off the platform and shone the torch to survey his handiwork. Then he reached to the clip at his belt; Jade had not noticed the riding crop that hung there. By the light of his lamp, the man slashed his fearsome scourge across Jade's straining thighs. She screamed in utter shock at the ferocious pain, leaping and dancing upon her toes as incredible waves of agony engulfed her. The second cut flamed into her belly, and the third, mercifully lighter than the other blows, seared across her soft breasts.

Then he was gone. Jade was left chained on her feet, alone in the pitch darkness, her flesh burning and tormented. For the rest of the night she had to stand in the darkness with her naked flesh against the rough stone walls, listening to sounds of ravishment from other cells.

Some days later, Jade was taken from the Dungeon. The Head Valet - escorting another naked, weeping young woman at the time - stopped at her cell, unlocked the gate, and ordered Jade out. Then he thrust the newcomer into the recess and relocked the gate.

"Your quarantine period is over," he told Jade. "You are to be presented to the Host."

Jade had learned not to ask questions. She reasoned that the letter Q, so prominently displayed on her breast, prevented the valets from fucking her. Those men and women who had been so used were usually only incarcerated in the dungeon for short periods and their breasts had not been marked. Jade shuddered, realising that she, too, would be regularly subjected to ravishment now that her quarantine was over. Secretly, the thought even thrilled her.

She followed the man up the spiral stairway and into the main building, along a labyrinth of corridors to a bathing annexe where the atmosphere was steamy and clammy. A naked woman waited there.

"She is to be washed, perfumed and prepared for presentation to the Host," ordered the Head Valet, thrusting Jade forward. "Shave her and fit a red collar."

Jade looked up sharply but did not protest. The young woman wore a green band about her neck. Her mound was unshaven and a thick, dark bush virtually concealed the cleft there. When she turned towards the shower area, Jade noticed that the girl's back was crisscrossed with fading red marks. They both stood beneath a gushing faucet while the Head Valet stood back.

"What place is this?" Jade whispered as the woman soaped her body. "How long have you been here?"

The woman made no reply as she massaged lather into Jade's breasts and between her thighs. The only sound for some moments was the gushing of the shower head.

"Why must I be shaven?" Jade asked presently, spluttering under the shower.

"Please," the girl whispered, glancing anxiously over her shoulder, "they do not allow us to speak. It is the rule that certain women are shaven. They are the special ones."

"Special?"

"I don't know. Shut up or they will beat us."

Later, Jade lay still and allowed the girl to carefully remove all trace of hair from her highly-slit pudenda. The attendant gasped but made no comment when Jade's large jutting clitoris was fully revealed. Make-up was expertly applied, both to face and denuded sex. Red, satin-covered, high-heeled mules were slipped onto her feet. Finally a self-locking, red-enamelled collar was fixed around her neck. The click as it closed seemed curiously final.

Jade stood for inspection and the Head Valet carefully appraised her. Satisfied, he took her wrists and confined them behind her back. The bath attendant draped a knee-length red cape about her shoulders and buckled it at her throat. The garment was completely open at the front and parted to reveal her long lissome limbs and naked body as she was hurried across the lawns.

"When you meet the Host, you must cooperate fully and display yourself at all times. Is that clear?"

"Yes, Master," Jade heard herself reply.

Heart pounding, she stood as prettily as she could contrive, blushing under the scrutiny of the Host. The presence of the beautiful Spanish woman made Jade's ordeal all the more humiliating. She now stood, naked but for satin mules, her head held high and erect, hip turned with her right knee slightly flexed and toes pointed. The shaving of her pubic mound fully revealed Jade's unusual petal-like nether lips and she felt more naked than ever. The protrusion of her large, pink clitoris was even more pronounced now.

"This one is quite beautiful," Serita declared.

The Host did not speak for some minutes as he frankly gazed upon Jade's young body.

"Her breasts are too small," Serita said.

The Host frowned. Jade struggled not to flinch as he reached out to heft each breast in turn. "True," he mused. "Perhaps that can be corrected."

"But she has at least one rare asset," Serita said, stooping to part Jade's sex lips.

The Host knelt on one knee to examine the morsel that nestled there more closely, and Jade blushed hotly. Then he straightened and said, as if to a child:

"There is no escape - you should understand that. Your role is to obey without question and there are no decisions for you to make. You are completely free to become the slut you yearn to become. In fact, we require it. You are quite pretty, Jade, but that is not enough. We will transform you into a superb and exquisite creature. Your body will be constantly available for our pleasure. Now that your quarantine period is over and the medical tests have been confirmed, you must attend our guests as we instruct. Fully! Do you understand?"

"Yes, sir." Jade whispered.

The Host turned to Serita. "If you would excuse us now, my dear."

The Spanish woman smiled and, with a last disdainful look at the nude woman, left the room. Jade watched fearfully as the Host produced a mask of purple, green and yellow feathers from a drawer in his desk. She stood rigid, frightened, as he tightly strapped the contraption about her head. Strategically placed pads muffled her ears and fitted snugly against her eyes, denying sound and vision.

Then Jade's body leapt as she discovered, like so many before her, that the master of that secret island preferred to personally initiate newcomers into service. Fingers wrenched her sex open, probing the flesh there. Then hands were at her breasts, tugging at her nipples, squeezing, plumping up the soft flesh. Jade gasped under his expert handling. Despite herself, she quickly became aroused and knew that her clitoris, teased by skilful fingers, had grown to prominent erection.

In the darkness, without hearing, Jade's whole being was focused upon the sexual epicentre of her body. A tide was rising relentlessly within her belly and, ultimately, after a long time, it exploded in a massive orgasm which left her weak and lifeless. Within seconds the Host reached his own climax, and Jade's aching body was buffeted as he furiously rode out his pleasure.

Later, the Host removed the mask and Jade, thoroughly used, found herself readmitted to the world of sight and sound. Her body was mottled and incredibly sensitive, both as a result of her sensory deprivation and the Host's skilled touch.

The Head Valet returned to collect his charge. Jade bowed her head shyly under his knowing smile as affixed the red cape about her shoulders.

"I am very pleased with you, little Jade," the Host called as she left.

"Thank you, sir," she was amazed to hear herself reply.

Outside, in the gardens, Jade shivered slightly even though the sun was shining brightly. The Head Valet suddenly grasped her by the neck, pushing downwards.

"Second rights are mine!" He forced Jade to her knees. "On all fours. Press your tits on the ground. Quickly now."

Jade, conditioned to obey, leaned forward to lay her breasts on the prickly grass. As the Head Valet intended, when the cape was tossed over her head the slave's buttocks were raised invitingly. She gasped beneath the cape as he took her swiftly from behind, his large weapon bludgeoning into her already moist womanhood. He gave no concession to her needs but merely satiated his own lust. Thus it was quickly over and Jade was scarcely breathing heavily when she rose to her feet. Suddenly, she found anger rising within her. How dare he treat her like this, like an animal?

Jade trembled with rage as he again tied the red cape about her shoulders and ordered her to walk ahead of him. She suddenly kicked out, deliberately and viciously, catching the man squarely in the testicles with considerable force. It was a telling blow despite her bare feet. He clutched his groin and fell to the ground with a strangled yell. Oh God, what had she done? It was too late to undo her action! After pausing to kick the writhing form once more, she darted off, running as if her very life depended upon it.

An old woman, clad entirely in black and wearing a head scarf, ambled by and hardly looked at the girl who sped past her. Then Jade saw a group of young women, all clad in short, deeply-slashed white tunics, toiling in the sun under the whip of a demanding overseer. The women were tending a large plot of vegetables and they strained to haul heavy water containers along the serried ranks of vegetation.

And, on the veranda of a large villa, another young woman, on hands and knees, scrubbed the white, marble stone. She, too, was clad in a short work tunic, and it rode up over her naked buttocks. Jade ran on, fearfully glancing over her shoulder. No one seemed to be giving chase yet. Darting up a narrow alley between two ramshackle buildings, the panting girl paused, leaning against rough walls and trying to regain some strength. When she had recovered a little, she climbed on a garbage bin and looked over the high wall.

The landscape behind the village was scorched and barren and, as far as she could tell, there were no other buildings. A rocky incline swept up to precipitous mountains. There was little choice: Jade hoisted herself over the wall and began to scramble up the hill. She picked her way through the rocky outcrops, trying to make use of what little cover there was, her red cape like a beacon under the harsh sunlight.

She climbed onwards and upwards until she could shelter in a small cave that was partially obscured by a scrubby and stunted tree.

She had escaped!

CHAPTER EIGHT

"Jade has escaped," Sebastian whispered to Sally as they waited in the training room.

"Escaped? That is not possible!"

"Ssh!" The Head Valet had entered, accompanied by Lily who was clad in a short white tunic.

Each morning, fed and watered, the slaves reported, naked, to the training rooms. Their daily exercise was quite as arduous as those enforced runs around the tunnel of the Dungeon. And there was other instruction; they were taught erotic arts they had scarcely thought existed. Valets attended their every move, instructing, cajoling, whips always at the ready.

"Posture!" the Head Valet called, and immediately the slaves snapped to attention, shoulders back, heads up and staring straight ahead.

Lily, too, her anxiety betrayed by the sharp rise and fall of her breasts straining against the thin cotton material of her short tunic. The Head Valet idly lifted her skirt with the butt of his whip. "What is your purpose?" he demanded

"To serve," Lily replied in a whisper.

He rapped her thighs sharply with the whip, demanding again: "What is your purpose?"

"To serve!"

"Good. Strip. Sebastian, Gunther, come here. The rest of you, form a circle, kneeling."

The women scurried to obey as the two male slaves padded forward with some diffidence. Lily stripped off her tunic and eyed first Sebastian and then Gunther. Their cocks hung limply as they stood awaiting instruction.

"Walk, Lily! The rest of you, watch and learn."

Obediently, Lily began to parade around the perimeter of the circle formed by the watching slaves. She walked with an exaggerated sway of her hips and, lowering her lashes, glanced seductively over her shoulder towards the waiting men. She lasciviously caressed her full breasts, teasing the long brown nipples. It was a consummate performance and, unmistakably, Sebastian and Gunther began to respond. Sally watched in fascination as Lily slowly began to caress the two nude men, wrapping her arms seductively about first one and then another. The male slaves, their cocks straining now, looked uncertainly towards the Head Valet.

"Enjoy!" he said with a slight smile.

The two men began to return Lily's caresses, hesitantly at first and then with assurance. Sometimes, she whispered an instruction. Quite suddenly, with fierce ardour, Gunther grasped the pliant woman and lifted her like a doll. The muscular German carried her high and she groaned in capitulation as she draped her legs over his shoulders, pressing her sex against his probing tongue. She was writhing and twisting by the time he lowered her to the floor.

Demanding now, urgently begging and pleading. she was rolled over by Sebastian's sturdy bare foot and hoisted to hands and knees. Immediately Gunther swooped to sink his rampant member into her now-sodden slit, and she moaned blissfully. Sebastian knelt expectantly in front of her wildly tossing head, and Lily took his erect penis into her mouth.

The girls watched with baited breath as she performed wholly and expertly. A heady aroma of feminine arousal unmistakably scented the air as the men took Lily with fervent, bludgeoning passion. Her body leapt rapturously beneath their onslaught, eagerly embracing the ravishment. Soon she was almost screaming in transports of ecstasy. Her body was mottled and suffused with an almost crimson hue. Sally Clark watched the exhibition with her mouth agape.

Sally's mind would not settle after seeing the shameful exhibition in the training room. The heat they had aroused in Lilly! And the heat it had aroused in Sally herself! She had not previously realised or even considered that such fierce and overwhelming needs could even be nurtured in a woman, much less that they could be so calculatedly unleashed to render her an abject helpless slave who begged piteously for satiation and release. Could they do this to her? Could the valets somehow nurture such irresistible and debasing appetites in her body? She trembled with the realisation that, ominously, her sex was almost dripping with helpless excitement. Well, could her captors inflict such abandoned degradation upon her, too? She discovered the answer some days later.

"Kneel," Serita ordered when she delivered Sally to the guest's room.

Sally knelt immediately, gazing around the apartment as her hands were manacled behind her back, but not daring to look at the guest. Serita's feet nudged the nude slave's knees apart, and Sally instantly parted her thighs as widely as she could, consciously revealing her sex. Then she steeled herself as her buttocks were spread across her heels by Serita's cool hands. Back ramrod straight, head bowed, Sally saw those little hands flutter to her breasts and she remained utterly still as Serita teased and tugged at the nipples, urging them into hard erection. She dare not protest, nor even speak, for it was forbidden.

"This is Sally," Serita told the man.

"You may look at me, girl," he said.

Sally looked up shyly and saw the man gazing candidly down, his eyes lingering on her spread nether lips. Could he see the moisture there? He smiled and reached into the pocket of his jacket; slowly, very deliberately, he drew out two small golden objects, each of which he dangled for the slave's gaze. They were almost like heavy, pendant earrings. Then he reached down and took Sally's right nipple, already as hard as a button after Serita's handling. He pulled at the engorged flesh until it throbbed and then also gathered the dimpled halo between his thumb and forefinger. Then, with a practised movement, he placed one of the cold gold objects over the soft flesh and Sally almost cried out as the teeth snapped shut. But she remained silent as he similarly treated her left nipple, quickly gathering the dark flesh and allowing tiny jaws to snap about it, making her gasp in agony.

The gleaming pendants now hung from her nipples and they felt very heavy upon her breasts. Almost immediately, the nipples began to throb insistently, concentrating Sally's whole awareness there. She arched her back and the guest laughed as he tugged first at one clamp and then at the other. As he pulled, Sally felt the little jaws tighten. She closed her eyes.

"Ingenious little things," the guest said to Serita. "Tension irreversibly tightens the grip. See?" Another sharp tug made Sally moan and almost wrenched her forward.

Then, pulling on the clamps, the man steadily and inexorably drew her forward and down. She whimpered but dare not desist. She heard the metal clamps clink upon the marble floor and felt her breasts rest upon the cold surface. Her spread buttocks were now raised higher than her head. She could no longer see either the man or Serita.

"This is an irritant but harmless," she heard the man say, "and it arouses a fierce need."

Then Sally gave a small squeal of surprise as a cold, slick, unyielding object nuzzled against her anus. The tight sphincter opened and she squirmed as a hard rod was gradually worked into her body. Her nipple clamps tapped against the marble floor and her bottom wriggled as the oiled, wide phallus slid into her reluctant flesh. When the man pulled her upright onto her knees, she felt the rod stretching and filling her rear. And it was beginning to burn - no, less fierce than burning, but definitely hot and persistent. Sally's eyes opened wide.

"Ah, it is beginning to take effect," the man said.

Then Sally's body jumped as his fingers spread her sex lips and smeared the oil there. The unguent, whatever it was, immediately began to tease and torment her. It was not an itch, not quite. The sensation defied description. How she wished for his cock inside her as she ground her hips and felt the huge phallus in her anus. Her nipples throbbed in harmony with the erotic charge below. She gasped as she tried to grind her gaping, dripping sex upon the cool marble floor.

"Excellent!" The guest stroked Sally's cheek. "Do you want us to satisfy your need, my little beauty?"

Forbidden to speak, she nodded wildly, tears of frustration and shame coursing down her cheeks. She could smell her own arousal.

"Bring the man."

Sally dared a glance upwards and she saw Serita leading the slave Sebastian by a leash. Nipple-clamps dangled from his bronzed chest and his cock was hugely erect, its pink head glistening. He, too, was in a state of anguished arousal but, like Sally, his hands were confined behind his back. It was evident that Sebastian had also been treated with the mysterious unguent, for his loins gave little twitches and his cock jerked spasmodically.

Oh, that cock! How she yearned for it inside her. She looked up piteously, first at Serita and then at the smiling guest, her eyes pleading, ignoring the stricture not to look into their faces.

"Artful little bitch," the man laughed, but he mercifully allowed the slave's ravishment.

Ordered to lower her shoulders and raise her buttocks once more, Sally groaned with satisfaction as Sebastian's thick cock entered her ready slit. There was no foreplay to arouse her - the unguent accomplished that - and the massive, demanding cock immediately pistoned inside her.

Wildly!

Painfully!

But it eased the maddening irritation for both Sebastian and for Sally. They were grinding against each other, bucking and moaning. Sebastian was intent upon burying every fraction of his tortured penis inside the woman's soaking and slippery flesh.

Yet the fierce burning around Sally's clitoris persisted; no matter how he fucked her, there was little relief there, merely an increased, persistent heat that almost drove her insane.

Sebastian was magnificent. He rode and pummelled Sally's flesh like an insatiable stallion. She was tossed like a rag doll and his plunging cock became the centre of her being. It seemed to last for an eternity, delicious and animalistic.

Sebastian's nipple-clamps beat rhythmically against Sally's shoulders as his heavy balls slammed against her bottom. She twisted and writhed beneath the exquisite onslaught and thrust back to meet his lust.

When her orgasm eventually came it was accompanied by a huge roar from Sebastian. He stiffened and, with one last deep plunge, Sally felt a spurt of hot semen within her vagina and the spent couple collapsed to the ground.

"Slut!" Serita stooped to grasp a hank of Sally's tousled hair and pulling the slave's head so that she could look into the flushed, tear-streaked face. "You stink!"

A heady aroma of sex pervaded the room. Sally was suddenly shy and she could not look at Sebastian. He, too, was strangely subdued now.

Valets were summoned and Sally and Sebastian were led away to the showers. For Sally, mercifully, there was an icy-cold douche to remove the still-burning irritant from her vagina. And the valets applied a soapy purge to Sebastian. He seemed to accept it gratefully and Sally later discovered that his anus as well as his penis had been treated with the irritant.

Jade, free but lost on the scorched Greek mountain side, was afraid and barely clinging to sanity. Cuts and scrapes bloodied her bare feet and legs. Even her buttocks were badly grazed after slithering down a rocky scree.

She was desperately thirsty.

Somewhere in this barren waste there must be a stream or river. On the previous day she had managed to find a small clear spring which bubbled up from a little fissure in the rocks, but since then she had not had a drop to drink. The presence of gorges told her that a flow of water had cut deeply into the rocks, but perhaps that was just in winter. At dusk on the previous day she had seen smoke rising to the west. Jade reasoned that where there was life there must also be water.

She scrambled on westwards. Sure enough a last she came upon a stream of sorts: barely a trickle, but clear and cold, enough to satisfy her thirst and, even, to wash the blood from her feet, legs and thighs. Jade had no container to carry water, of course, and she had no wish to find herself in a similar predicament again. So she decided to follow the stream downwards. After perhaps a mile or so, breathless and sweating, she was delighted when the stream widened into a large irregularly-shaped pool, surrounded by rocks and fed by two or three similar small tributaries. A natural reservoir. Jade threw off her cape and gratefully plunged into the cool water.

She swam for some minutes in the deep pool, forgetting everything that had gone before and almost oblivious to her surroundings. Then, to her horror, she saw a figure strolling beside the pool. Hurriedly, she pulled herself behind an overhanging rock and lowered herself deeper into the water.

It seemed that the man had not seen her, although he certainly noticed her red cape as it lay on the ground; he picked up the garment, examined it at arms length, shrugged, and tucked it under his arm, strolling back the way he had come.

"Hey, you're cheating."

"God, you scared me!" Jade exclaimed, her heart pounding with shock as she saw a young man surface behind her.

"You should be scared. If they find you hiding instead of working it will be a whipping in Big Hall, at the very least, perhaps a week in the Dungeon even. Besides, it isn't fair on the rest of us."

"What are you doing here?"

The handsome young man laughed. "Hiding for a while, just like you," he said. "I wanted to avoid that big ugly brute among them. Into total degradation and humiliation, that one. Well, I've done my stint with him - let someone else have the pleasure today."

Jade forced a smile. "I'm avoiding him too."

"Let's fuck."

"What?"

"Yeah. Why not? That's what we're here for, after all. No good being coy now, so we may as well enjoy ourselves."

With that the man pulled Jade to him in the water and she felt his hard cock nuzzling against her thighs. He kneaded her soft breasts as he kissed her. She did not struggle. Somehow, it seemed inadvisable, if this is what the slaves did...

The young man was an amazingly gentle and skilled lover. Despite everything, despite herself, Jade became aroused as he relentlessly caressed her large clitoris. They made long, languorous love and she groaned as his organ slid into her yielding flesh. Afterwards, they both lay back in the water.

After some minutes the man clearly became nervous and fretful. He constantly looked over her shoulder and peeped around the rocks.

"I think it is safe now," he said. "The ugly brute is groping and rolling with the Scandinavian twins. Come on, let's go back."

"I'm not going back!"

The man, collared like her, spoke in astonishment: "Of course you have to go back. There is no escape, you know that."

"I have to try!"

"When they find that you have gone missing, it will be a whipping and the rat-hole for the rest of us. They use peppered punishment phalluses on the guys. I am not about to risk that again - I'll report you to the valet if necessary. Are you coming back or not?"

"Well -" Jade considered the situation. "Yes, yes, alright!"

"Attagirl!" He laughed as they started to swim around the rock. "You're new aren't you? I could tell when we made love. Make a bee-line for the little Arab with the gold rings - he was quite gentle with me last night."

The sight that confronted Jade on the far bank of the pool was unbelievable. Some twenty or so naked men and women splashed in the water or lolled about on the surrounding rocks, carousing with eight or nine guests. A couple of small jeeps and three covered donkey-carts stood on a track above the gorge - obviously the party's means of conveyance to this remote spot.

"Do you often come here?" Jade asked the man as her feet found the rocky shelf and she began to walk walk to the side, her naked breasts above the water line.

"They've brought here me a couple of times before. You?"

"Like you said, I'm new."

"Hey, look over there. See what I mean?"

The man pointed to a rocky platform overhanging the water. A large balding man was tormenting a beautiful blonde woman. The writhing girl had been tied, on her back, to the bare roots of a scrubby tree: the rope which bound each ankle had been passed under a stout root behind her head and tightened so that both legs were held splayed about a foot from the ground. It was an inventive tie, because each time she attempted to lower one leg, then the other was forced higher into the air. To relieve the pressure, the girl was forced to bend her knees and widen her thighs, opening herself. The man was beating the inside of her soft thighs with a strap and she kicked like a puppet on string. Compounding the degradation, another blonde woman sat astride her mouth.

"Those twins certainly get their share," the man said matter-of-factly. "He'll beat her until she makes her sister come. Then he'll screw the pair of 'em - his stamina is something else, I can tell you. The Arab is over there, see?"

Jade found herself grabbed by the arm and pulled towards a small darkskinned fellow who was lying idly in the shallow water at the pool's edge. He was being attended by a young black girl with massive, swinging breasts.

"What's your name?"

"Sue. But -"

"Sir, I have someone who is dying to meet you, Sir. She is a specialist in your preferred pleasure. This is Sue."

Jade, standing ankle-deep in the clear water, blushed as the man's keen eyes roved over her naked body. He noted the cuts and abrasions on her legs. "Someone has been rather overzealous with you, eh?"

"Yes."

He waved the pouting black girl away, saying, "Come, Sue, lay with me. We shall indulge in your speciality."

With an inward groan Jade stretched in the water beside the man. He waited expectantly, smiling broadly. A valet sauntered nearby and looked quizzically in her direction. Would he realise that she was not part of his original group? Surely, they had some notion of who had and had not been brought here? Whether it was her imagination or not, Jade could feel the valet's eyes scrutinising her. Unless she did something to entertain the smiling Arab, then he, too, might make a scene which she could ill-afford.

She rolled onto the swarthy-skinned little man, grabbing him and continuing the roll until he was lying on top of her in the water, obscuring the view of the valet. The man seemed surprised. Jade feigned eagerness, clawing his back and wrapping her strong thighs about him. Her tongue thrust deeply into his throat. When she allowed him a respite, his large member

64

was already swelling between her thighs.

He laughed. "So that is your speciality?"

"Anything."

With a movement as sudden as that with which Jade first surprised the man, he turned her. She gasped and spluttered as he briefly held her head below the water. His knees were between hers, roughly forcing them apart, and his hands were under her belly. The small man was surprisingly strong, and his now erect member was astonishingly big. He hoisted her belly upwards until she was kneeling, shoulders still pressed into the rock, and with her bottom thrust out towards him.

"This, pretty Sue, is my speciality!" She gave a small squeal of pain and surprise as he thrust his member into her tight rear orifice.

Panting, shifting her bottom slightly to ease the passage of the thrusting member, Jade raised her head and gazed through the curtain of wet hair which now covered her face. The valet was smiling in their direction as he turned away. Then Jade was obliged to devote her whole attention and her body to the plundering Arab.

Presently, thoroughly rutted and ravaged, she lay in the shallow water, attempting to ease her soreness. Contrary to the promise made by the young male slave, this small, swarthy character had not been at all gentle. A quick survey of the debauchery occurring around her, however, made Jade realise that the assessment was relative.

"You are too tight there," the Arab complained.

Jade shrugged. She saw that the bald man had now forced one of the Scandinavian twins to lie on the other, and he was alternately pumping his massive penis into first one and then the other of the offered vaginas. Elsewhere, a woman was precariously bridged between two standing men, her back was arched as she was anchored between two rampant male organs, one of which impaled her sex whilst the other was thrust in her mouth. The handsome young fellow who had brought her to the Arab was now rolling in the arms of another man.

"Food, Master?" a woman asked, wading into the water and carrying a tray of succulent meats.

The Arab took a couple of roasted chicken legs and waved the woman away. He took a bite from one drumstick, and then tossed the other in the air. Jade scrambled for the scrap, desperate to catch it before it landed in the water, and then she gnawed every piece of meat from the bone.

"I must relieve myself," Jade told the Arab, before swimming across the pool.

Once out of sight behind the rocky outcrop, she hauled herself from the water. She would do anything to avoid falling into the clutches of these people again! She fled up the hill, stark naked now.

CHAPTER NINE

Jade was naked, cold and hungry. In the light of morning, she had to make a decision. She could not stand another night in the wilds. Her endurance had reached its limits. She sat huddled in a small abandoned cabin, in a deep mountain rift. On the previous night, a cold wind had howled through the gorge, whipping through the cabin's cracked timbers.

What now?

That decision was quickly made for her: the rickety door burst open and a small ragged urchin stood gazing into the cabin. Jade warily approached the door and looked anxiously outside. No-one else was there. It seemed the boy was alone except for a herd of skinny goats grazing on sparse scrub. Returning to the cabin, she gratefully snatched the battered tin flask that the lad silently offered. Drinking thirstily, she asked, "Food? Do you have any food?"

He understood and produced a hunk of bread and grubby cheese from a hessian bag slung over his shoulder. There was silence for some minutes and the lad watched in fascination as Jade hungrily wolfed the food. Presently, she asked: "Can you find me some clothes, boy?"

He looked at her uncomprehendingly. Jade repeated the question in French and German, but still he did not understand. She tugged the lapel of his tattered shirt. "Clothes! Clothes!"

The boy grinned widely.

"Clothes, women's clothes" - Jade gestured expansively towards her bare breasts - "yes?"

"Ah!" Suddenly he scurried from the cabin.

"And food!" Jade called after him. "More food."

She followed the boy from the shack and was surprised to see that he was already climbing the steep side of the gorge. His goats still munched at the sparse vegetation around the cabin, so he would return. Hopes raised, Jade again sought shade inside the shack. With clothing and, perhaps, some food, then there might be a chance after all.

Heartened, she fell asleep. Later, a foot nudged her rudely into consciousness. She looked up and saw the boy and, standing beside him, a handsome tanned man. Jade crossed her arms across her breasts as he eyed her intently.

The boy spoke animatedly, but the man gestured that he be silent. "You are the English woman," he said. "They look for you with a helicopter."

Jade nodded. She had spent the past two days diving for cover whenever she heard the whirring of an engine. "Yes," she said, "Do you have clothes for me?"

"They are very powerful people."

"Yes, very bad. My husband is a rich man..."

The man removed his own shirt and handed it to Jade. Gratefully she pulled it over her shoulders. The muscles of his chest and shoulders rippled in the dappled light which filtered through the cracked boarding of the shack.

"Come. I take you."

"Where? To your home? You are taking me to your home?"

The man nodded and said something in Greek to the young boy, who clapped his hands with glee and ran from the hut.

"He must tend the goats. We go."

The rough shirt scarcely covered Jade's bottom but even that was a luxury. She cheerfully followed the man from the cabin. However, when he began to climb the steep, rocky sides of the gorge, Jade hesitated, squinting up at the frightening heights above. He grinned, held out his hand, and effortlessly hauled her to the first foothold. The climb was arduous but she followed courageously. At one particularly hazardous point, the man pushed her ahead with strong, firm hands that cupped her naked buttocks. She was acutely aware that the shirt hid little and that he was excited by what he saw.

At the top of the rocky gorge there were more rocks. She gasped in horror.

"Lady no worry." He sat on a ledge and patted the ground beside him.

Jade sat beside the man. "How much further?"

He smiled. "Not far. You are very beautiful. I see why they hunt you."

"My husband is very wealthy and strong. He loves me very much."

The man shrugged. "He is not here."

With that, he leapt to his feet and began to climb once more. Now the climb was less demanding and Jade found it relatively easy to follow the handsome stranger. Here was a man who, on this island, seemed different: he made no demands, despite her helpless condition.

"What is your name?" she asked.

"They call me Zorba. It is not my name but it will do."

Zorba took Jade to his home: a poor hovel in the heart of the mountains.

Eagerly she ate a meal of moussaka. It was good. Zorba explained that he had worked as a cook in a taverna before the island was purchased by the 'organisation'.

"You must bathe," he counselled, and his tone of authority irritated Jade.

Nevertheless, a galvanised tub was filled with hot water. It seemed pointless now to hide her naked body from Zorba. Anyway, the man made no attempt to force himself upon her, despite his frank gaze. Jade stripped and lowered herself into the water. As an afterthought, she took the opportunity to rinse the dirty shirt which remained her only garment.

She began to feel safe and secure in the dilapidated little house with its vine-clad veranda. The boy, Andreas, returned briefly to snatch a mid-morning meal before dashing off again.

When Zorba left for work at midday, Jade was busily scrubbing and dusting, something which she had never done since marrying John Preston. It would be late evening before Zorba returned, she reasoned. However, he came back in less than one hour, accompanied by three other men. Jade did not even hear them coming: the door suddenly opened and there they stood.

She gasped in disbelief and horror. Zorba had betrayed her! He stood, unsmiling, alongside the man they called the Head Valet.

"Strip."

Jade looked around wildly, but the men barred the only exit. Lunging forward, she tried to dart between them but the men were too quick. They roughly hurled her back, and she fell on the tiles.

"Strip!"

Defeated, Jade rose to her feet. She tossed her head and, staring defiantly at Zorba, unbuttoned the coarse shirt. The garment fell open, revealing her naked body. With a shrug, she allowed it to slip to the floor. One of the valets produced a pair of stout handcuffs and fastened Jade's hands behind her. Then, quite unnecessarily, he also manacled her ankles. She would not escape again.

So it is done, she thought. Captured!

The Head Valet approached and grasped Jade's hair, forcing her head back. "You will pay dearly for the trouble you have caused," he said. "I will make it my personal business to ensure that you become the most docile, submissive and degraded slut on the island."

She spat in his face. The other men barely suppressed their amusement and exchanged delighted smiles. Jade yelped in pain as the Head Valet's whip crashed down upon her shoulders. She thought her jaw would break as they pushed a pierced leather ball behind her teeth and secured it tightly with a strap. Not content with that, a leather mask was strapped around her eyes.

Chained, gagged, and blindfolded, Jade was dragged from the house and bundled into an open-top jeep. They fastened her wrists to the vehicle's anti-roll bar above her head.

The journey over steep mountains and unmade tracks was an unpleasant one for the captured woman. Although a hole in the gag allowed her to breathe, the leather pressed painfully against her teeth and jaw. Sightless, she was unprepared for the jolts and sudden swerving turns as the jeep negotiated the rocky terrain. Moreover, she was repeatedly tormented with spiteful flicks of the Head Valet's whip that continuously stung her belly, arms and breasts.

Jade was taken straight to the Doctor's surgery on her return to the complex. She had gained some notoriety: the special acquisition who had virtually maimed the Head Valet and escaped. It had been unheard of for a woman to abscond; precautions were not normally considered to be very important, but the Head Valet was acutely embarrassed by the whole affair. The woman's blows, to both his body and his pride, had made him the butt of much amusement. For days he had quietly seethed. Now he would obtain his satisfaction and recover lost stature.

"Make sure she is fit for punishment," he told the Doctor.

"Very well. Unchain her and remove the gag and blindfold."

"No."

The Doctor looked up in surprise. "I can hardly examine her as she is," he protested.

"You can see enough."

Jade's medical examination was less than thorough and the Doctor pronounced her fit but disclaimed responsibility. Without further ado, the Head Valet ordered that she be taken to the basement.

"Leave the gag in place," he said sharply as the duty valets rose to process the newcomer.

Even in the dim lighting of the cellar, Jade blinked when the blindfold was removed from her eyes. She looked wildly about her and grimaced as the Head Valet's whip once more bit into her buttocks. Then they removed the cuffs from her hands and replaced them with leather bracelets. A leather collar replaced the red enamelled one, and her wrists were secured to it before the valet, standing warily behind her, removed her ankle chains.

"Hose her down."

Valets dragged Jade to a bare little room where the walls and floor were constantly wet. Thrust to the far wall, she screeched as an icy blast of water splattered painfully against her body. Twisting and turning, she struggled in the force of the gush, trying to protect her aching breasts. Shivering with cold, she was dragged back into the basement.

"No showers for her," the Head Valet instructed, pleased by Jade's discomfort. "She is to be hosed down daily. Now, whip her from shoulders to calves. Thoroughly. Understand?"

The whipping applied to Jade was indeed thorough. The duty valet knew that it broke the rules but he dare not object. When it was finished, the sobbing woman was utterly chastened and ready to obey any command.

"Run her around the tunnel until she drops," the Head Valet ordered.

The man looked up in surprise but he saw the grim expression on the face of his superior. He nodded and pushed Jade, stumbling, through the dungeon door. She grunted behind the gag as knotted thongs seared across her belly. The valet pushed her roughly forward.

"Run. Knees up."

Reluctantly at first, and then faster in a vain bid to escape the vicious whip, Jade began to run along the tunnel. She paid little heed to the order to raise her knees, but sprinted ahead. After completing the first circuit, another valet was waiting to take over.

"Run!" the second man commanded. "Knees up."

Sobbing, Jade again sped away and she managed to keep sufficiently far ahead of her pursuer to avoid his swishing lash. All around the tunnel, men and women stood at the bars of their cells, watching. After two laps, she was slowing and the first valet, rested now, stood waiting to take up the chase.

No matter how fast she ran, the punishing leather repeatedly slapped against her thighs, her buttocks, calves. The valets were calculating and expert with their blows. Sobbing, running wildly, sometimes hopping, seemingly lifted by the lash, Jade struggled to complete a third circuit of the long tunnel. This time the waiting valet held a long leather lash, and it caught her across the belly as she passed.

"Knees up. Get those knees up!" He curled the lash across her shoulders as he took up the chase.

Jade's lungs ached and breath rasped her throat. She slowed. Reluctantly, despising herself, she began to raise her knees as she ran. They would punish her for daring to escape and she knew that utter obedience was her only course now.

"Higher!"

She complied and ran in a prancing trot, somehow raising her leaden legs to waist height. The man was controlling her pace, she knew. Jade was grateful for the gag: without it, she would have begged for mercy.

Her torment went on for lap after lap of the dungeon tunnel. Inmates in the cells no longer watched and many huddled on their sleeping platforms. Jade became utterly exhausted yet the harrying valets relentlessly drove her on. Soon she was stumbling against the walls, falling, exhausted, but the men continually whipped her to her feet. Presently even the cruel lash could not revive her and she was dragged to an empty cell where they left her, a crumpled heap upon the cold stone floor.

Serita strolled into the dungeon to gaze at the stricken creature. There was a haughty, contemptuous smile upon her face. "So you have recaptured the animal who gave you so much trouble, eh?"

The Head Valet's small eyes narrowed. He did not like this arrogant Spanish woman. Nominally, she was subordinate to him, a trainee instructor. In reality, however, she was a confidante of the Host. Even the Head Valet dare not question Serita too much.

"She will be tamed, I promise you!"

"You know nothing," Serita sneered. "Give her to me and she will feed from my hand."

The Head Valet made no reply as the Spanish beauty strode away with a toss of her long black mane. The man's practised eye automatically assessed Serita: she had a pert rear, well defined by tight carefully-cut designer jeans. He wondered how she would look naked, chained and submissive, and he could imagine a pretty picture. How he would like to have Serita beneath his whip in the Dungeon, posing her nude for the guests who visited there!

CHAPTER TEN

Privileged quests often came to see the wretched inmates who were held, naked and abused, in the Dungeon. Natasha Tranter loathed them. She would not comply with the degrading demands they made. She would rather be beaten. And while, at first, the indignity of being publicly beaten had been an affront to her fierce pride and, thus, an exquisite punishment in itself, the novelty wore off. After all, every slave was naked here, and every one of them was beaten, so where was the shame in that? Her victory was in the stoical and almost contemptuous manner in which she took the beatings. Natasha rarely cried out.

This, she had decided, would be her rebellion. No man had ever mastered her. Not the powerful Felix Tranter, her husband, who usually managed to crush resistance from anyone who stood in his path. The Communist commissars had not mastered her, either. Nor would these men! So when a group of six visitors came to peer expectantly through the bars of her cell, Natasha remained supine upon the sleeping platform, facing the wall.

"Stand and present yourself!" the valet ordered.

Natasha glanced contemptuously over her shoulder, and adjusted her position slightly so that the main features of her nude body, those they wanted to see, were all but concealed.

"Stand!" the valet rasped again. "Hands on your head!"

Natasha did not move. It was as if she were lost in her thoughts and deaf to the barked commands. She kept telling herself that they would not break her. She heard the sound of the barred gate being unlocked and flung open. Then a hand roughly grasped her hair and dragged her from the platform.

"On your back," the valet yelled. "Present yourself for the guests."

This time Natasha merely looked up directly into his eyes and smiled defiantly. His cane whistled through the air and she arched involuntarily as it bit painfully into her back. She smiled. Again the cane beat down, causing her body to jerk but she remained on the floor. The beating was exceptionally long and severe and the visitors gazed on in salacious wonderment. Ten, eleven, twelve strokes. Now there was blood, a trace of blood on her thighs.

The valet became somewhat anxious: he had the licence to beat women, indeed was encouraged to do so, but the Host would deal severely with those who scarred his precious merchandise. The inmates must never be permanently damaged - that was the code and the captive's assurance. He lowered the cane and turned apologetically towards the guests.

"This one is not yet ready. Please choose another."

Triumphant for the while, although acutely sore, Natasha turned away and stretched gingerly upon her sleeping platform. It was not long before the night period, but Natasha found it hard to sleep in the pitch darkness of the Dungeon. Despite being naked and without any covering, it seemed unbearably hot and stuffy.

Then, in the inky-darkness, a dim beam of light reflected on wall opposite her cell. Gradually, the light became stronger. A hand-torch. And, yes, muted masculine voices. Natasha almost gagged in fear. Like the others, she had received many unscheduled visits from the valets, and several sound thrashings, purely for being there, it seemed. She huddled into a foetal position and feigned sleep, hoping they would go away.

In fact, the two men walked straight past Natasha's cell and, within a few moments, she heard the unlocking of a barred gate nearby, two or three cells beyond her own. A woman yelped, perhaps roughly awakened with a sharp rap of the cane. Natasha recognised the voice of the English woman, the one they called Jade. After some further minutes, the unmistakable sounds of copulation could be heard. The groans and grunts gradually rose in intensity, until the woman could clearly be heard screaming and begging.

Natasha was horrified. And yet, listening, she could tell that the slut Jade was not crying out in fear or pain: these cries were those of female arousal and surrender. The sounds went on for some considerable time and Natasha lay tossing and turning, unable to blot them out.

Quite unexpectedly, the Russian woman realised that she had become aroused herself. Perhaps it was not surprising, for her strong sexual appetites had not been relieved for many days. And now her wrists were fastened to the collar about her neck! The valets had never attempted to fully use her body. Instead, usually, they merely tied her to the bars and lashed her unmercifully with canes or whips or straps.

The next day, when the slaves turned out of their cells for the mandatory exercise run, as they stood to attention and awaited the sound of the whistle, Natasha strained to look at the women in front of her. Jade's naked back was not particularly marked or bruised. Why should it be? It was not as if the valets had raped or forced their victim in any way. Quite the contrary, she had clearly been begging for more.

Then the whistle sounded and, in time with the woman immediately in front, the line immediately set off in a prancing run, knees reaching to waist-height. Natasha, a trained gymnast and natural athlete, found no difficulty in these daily work-outs and her body was already beginning to shed those unwanted ounces which had accrued through indolence and indulgence.

Exercise concluded, the women went for a warm, luxurious shower. Not

Jade, though: the Head Valet insisted that she be hosed down by the fierce jet. After the hosing, strangely sore as if having been beaten, Jade would kneel on the sleeping platform and brush her hair. Even in these dank and miserable conditions, the valets insisted that appearances be maintained. One day, while brushing her hair, Jade became aware that she was being observed. She looked up and saw someone staring through the bars: it was Serita, the Host's special trainer, cool and immaculate in a cream safari-type suit and polished brown boots.

"Very pretty," Serita said. "Maintain that position."

Jade groaned inwardly. Kneeling, raised arms lifting her breasts, she presented an erotic sight.

"If you move without permission I will call the valets. You may call me Mistress."

There was something about the demeanour of this woman which stayed Jade's anger and she remained in the pose, the brush still lifted to her hair, as if frozen in time.

"Open your thighs," the woman demanded. "Wider! More!"

Jade obeyed. She continued to stare steadily ahead, as if mesmerised.

"Suck in your belly. It is too fat. Yes?"

A reply was obviously demanded and, after some hesitation - for the captives were warned to silence - Jade replied.

"Yes, Mistress."

"Mistress! Good. Very good. Perhaps I like you. Stand - no, keep your hands high. Now come to me. Closer. Yes, still closer. Place your hands through the bars, yes, grip the metal in the crook of your arms. Tightly. Yes. Now place your leg through the bars. Now the other leg. Bend your knees and clasp the bars. That is good."

Jade clung against the cold steel, her legs widely splayed through the bars, gripping with clasped hands to support herself. Her breasts protruded provocatively on either side of a stout unyielding rod.

"That's good!" The woman spoke soothingly, stroking the soft flesh. "Hold steady."

Jade was transfixed as the woman began to caress her inner thighs, reaching under her splayed and opened body. Then the fingers were delving into the soft flesh, parting her lips and teasing, tugging, twisting...

"No!" Jade murmured, although she did not resist.

"You cannot say that, little fool. Beg your mistress to continue."

Jade shook her head wildly, her eyes wide and a tortured groan emitted from her throat. Then the cruelly smiling woman thrust her fingers deeper into the moist flesh. Jade squirmed. Oh, no, not this, not a woman. But there she was, writhing under Serita's touch and gaining an exquisite forbidden pleasure that she could not understand.

"Yes! Please, Mistress. Yes!"

74

"Little slut!" Serita sneered, thrusting her fingers deep into Jade's slit. "You like? Serita will give you much pleasure. You obey your mistress, Serita, uh?"

"Yes, yes, anything!"

A passing valet paused as Jade ground her vagina down upon the invading digits, then continued on his way. Serita smiled cruelly as she inflicted pleasure upon her helpless victim. After merciful orgasm had overtaken Jade, her soft flesh remained crushed against the bars.

"Suck clean," Serita commanded, thrusting her fingers into Jade's mouth. "That was good? Yes, very good. You may thank your mistress."

"Th-thank you Mistress."

Quite suddenly, unexpectedly, Serita slapped one of Jade's breasts viciously with the palm of her hand. "So... I will return, little slut."

After the dark-haired beauty had gone, Jade wearily disentangled her limbs from the bars. She tossed her head, swishing long dishevelled tresses from her face, and returned to the sleeping platform. Kneeling there, knees widely spaced, she began again to brush her hair, adopting the pose which had so interested the haughty beauty.

This woman, Serita, had discovered another of Jade's weaknesses, and one that had been hidden from her until now. The cruel Serita, free and clothed while she, Jade, was naked and enslaved, had released unsuspected forces. Jade was neither shamed nor humiliated by the abuse. She was a willing and eager victim. It had been the same when valets so comprehensively used her body during the blackout period. It was, she knew, simply her nature, and in slavery it could not be denied.

Serita, the cruel mistress, had said that she would return. When? Jade looked down at the red print of the woman's small hand on her breast and tenderly caressed the mark, not to ease the pain but to savour it.

Serita Fernandez stretched languorously as the Host toyed idly with the dark nipple, almost black, that badged her breast. Her unblemished olive skin contrasted starkly with the white silk sheets.

"Enough!" she suddenly snapped.

"I am sorry, my dear," the Host murmured, desisting immediately.

"Cigarette?"

"Certainly."

Rising from the bed, still naked, he hurried across the room and returned bearing a silver box.

"Light it for me!" Serita ordered imperiously.

"As you wish," the Host said with a courtly bow. He took a cigarette from the box and placed it between his lips. A nonsmoker, he scarcely concealed his abhorrence as he lit the cigarette and inhaled.

"The undisputed master of all those creatures," Serita said contemptuously, "and you are nothing."

"It is as you say," the Host said, coughing slightly and handing the cigarette to the nude, reclining woman. "You are magnificent."

"And you are a despicable little worm. You have all of these slaves and yet you must serve me as your mistress. That is funny."

The Host hung his head but a smile flickered across his face. His limp member was beginning to become erect once again as he made to lie beside Serita. She viciously slapped the rising penis away and, instead, pushed his head downwards, opening her legs to reveal pink and moist sex lips nestling in a jet-black bush, the demand obvious.

The Host turned and knelt, head down between the tawny thighs. He began to lap avidly at the woman's exposed sex, tasting the tang of his own semen. Then, suddenly shocked, he leapt in pain as Serita ground the glowing cigarette into his naked buttock but, after only a moment, he continued to lick at her cunt. His erection grew to massive, throbbing proportions.

Later, in his office, the Host asked Serita: "You do understand the nature of our relationship, my dear? Things that happen in the privacy of my living quarters must never be allowed to interfere with the running of our organisation."

"Of course."

"The Head Valet tells me that the acquisitions are afraid of you?"

"I despise them. How they tolerate such degradation is a mystery to me."

The Host smiled. He had received regular reports on Serita's activities since her arrival on the island. The Head Valet had complained that she was arrogant and did not conform to the strict regime imposed upon the other instructors. Indeed, as the only woman trainer, Serita enjoyed a specialist role which allowed her to do pretty much as she wished. He had ordered that Serita Fernandez be excused from the mundane chores allotted to valets. This, of course, had not made the woman popular.

"You do not seem concerned by your long absence from your husband?"

"Carlos requires respectability and intelligence from his wife, and subservience from his whores. He has his stable of compliant females and that is enough for him. The man is a dolt."

The Host looked up, as if surprised, as her dark eyes flashed with obvious anger. "Senor Fernandez does not satisfy you in bed?"

"He would be only too pleased if I crawled to lick his feet like his enslaved sluts. Never! I would kill him. He cannot divorce me because I can destroy him. So our marriage is - it is convenient, that is all."

The Host smiled and kissed her hand. "I understand that you wish to supervise Jade's punishment. May I ask why?"

"I prepare a special surprise for you."

He raised his eyebrows quizzically. "Very well."

Serita laughed with delight. "I will commence my preparation of Jade tomorrow, after her morning exercise."

Jade completed her morning exercise as usual, submitted to the dreaded icy hoses, and returned to her cell. Two valets, however, had followed her, and she suddenly found herself flung, belly down, across the sleeping platform. Her legs flailed wildly as one of the men straddled her upper torso. His colleague lashed her exposed buttocks with his whip, immediately stilling her frenzied kicks.

"Open your legs," an accented female voice ordered.

Serita! Shamed, Jade parted her thighs. She buried her head in the mattress. The Spanish woman reached forward and pressed her finger into Jade's exposed anus until the sphincter opened.

"The Arab was correct," Serita said. "She is too tight. Proceed."

Jade suddenly screeched and writhed as a cold, hard object was introduced into her body. The valet ignored her howls of protest as he pushed home a short ebony rod. Jade felt the distending object being strapped to her body. Then it was over and the valets released her.

"Stand," ordered Serita.

Jade struggled to her feet, uncomfortably aware of the object firmly embedded in her body. Obeying Serita's gesture, she surveyed her image in the full-length mirror: thin leather straps, attached to a belt, passed between her legs on either side of her sex to secure the unyielding plug.

"It must only be removed by one of the valets. Understand, slut?"

The woman laughed and her hand mockingly caressed Jade's cheek. Then the barred gate was locked and Serita left with the valet.

Jade tried to loosen the uncomfortable rod, but it was tightly held. Standing before the mirror, she turned, bent and stretched to view her rear: a black, saddle-shaped object followed the contour of her body between the spread buttocks, terminating just above the opening of her sex. At the small of her back, a padlock dangled from the tightly buckled straps.

"Ah, you doubt my words."

Jade was startled to hear the Spanish woman's voice and she whirled around too see her smiling contemptuously through the bars.

"You are uncomfortable, uh? That is nothing. We will increase the stretch each day by inserting a wider plug. It is a kindness. Better you are stretched now. Thank your mistress for her kindness."

"Thank you, Mistress, for your k-kindness," Jade whispered.

For the next few days, even during exercise, Jade wore a plug in her anus. It was removed only twice daily, when she must relieve herself. Then she had to bend double, accepting the humiliation as one valet parted her buttocks while another inserted and harnessed the rod. Straps about her thighs and waist ensured that everyone who saw her knew that she wore the device. Jade was always acutely aware of the stretching sensation in her anus.

"Ah, my pretty slut!" Serita paused at the bars of Jade's cell. "How is the stretching progressing? Turn around and spread yourself. Good. That is a good girl."

Humiliated, Jade bent and held her buttocks apart. She jumped slightly as Serita twisted the rod.

"They change it daily for a larger one?"

"Yes, Mistress."

"It is good. You take a big man there, uh? Turn around, little one."

Jade straightened and turned. She was humiliated by the way this haughty woman spoke to her, like a small child, despite the similarity of their ages.

"You like sex with men, uh?"

"No, Mistress," Jade blurted.

"Ah, your eyes say that is not true. You suck valets' cocks?"

"Sometimes."

"I fetch a valet - someone you know."

Dismayed, Jade watched Serita stride purposefully away. Within minutes she returned, accompanied by Zorba. He grinned cheerfully and unlocked the barred gate.

"You suck cock now," Serita ordered. "I watch."

Oh, no, not Zorba! But the man she now knew to be a valet had already entered her cell. Reluctantly, she sank to her knees and began to fumble with the fastening of his breeches. His penis was already becoming erect. With a doe-eyed glance towards the smiling Serita, Jade obediently began to caress the member delicately with the tip of her tongue. Soon she was taking it deeply into her throat, eliciting sighs from the swaying Zorba.

"Little slut!" Serita sneered. "You like that? It is good?"

Jade swallowed deeply as Zorba's semen gushed forth. Rising, wiping her mouth with the back of her hand, she stood awaiting Serita's further instruction. However, the Spanish woman merely tutted contemptuously. Zorba shrugged and ruffled Jade's hair affectionately before leaving the cell.

"You like!" Serita accused when he had gone. "It is good, uh? Now I teach you other things. Stand up and spread your legs. Now bend over. Further. You are very stiff. Get your head down and look at me from between your legs. You see your prize clitoris, uh? Big and hungry, like no other. Slut! I come to you often after this. We will loosen your body and you will learn to stand like that, easily, perfectly."

Serita frequently attended Jade in the following days. Each time she insisted that the slave double her body, not satisfied until Jade could position her head directly below the open leaf-like lips of her sex. And, all the time,

Serita would handle her intimately, caressing, stroking and probing. Afterwards, always, a valet would be summoned, and Jade was required to suck his erect cock. Sometimes, just for the sake of it, Serita would whip Jade until her bare flesh glowed in fiery hues.

"I have a special treat for that hungry cunt of yours," Serita announced when she arrived one day, unlocking the barred gate. "Out!"

Jade sprang to her feet and hurried to stand in the narrow tunnel. A blindfold was tightly buckled upon her. It fitted snugly, allowing no light to pass. She groped sightlessly as Serita ushered her along the tunnel.

"Halt!"

The air was cold here. Jade heard the sound of a heavy lock turning.

"Forward."

Coarse masonry grazed her flanks as she walked. Then cold cobbles gave way to lush carpeting beneath her bare feet. She hesitated fretfully as Serita guided her down a flight of steps. Then she gasped, grasped by the hair and dragged forward into sudden warmth.

Thrust to her knees, Jade felt and heard a heavy chain being fixed to her collar; the cold hard links draped between her breasts. Then the blindfold was removed. She found herself closely-confined in a low-ceiling chamber. Despite the heat emitted by a large radiator, the room smelled of damp and musty air. Its walls were of bare rough-hewn rock but a thickly-piled red carpet covered the floor. There was no furniture, just a few cushions placed beyond her reach.

Because of the short chain that connected her collar to the wall, Jade could not stand. She was able to kneel, turn, crouch, lie on belly or back, but she could not stand upright. She was allowed briefly to survey her condition before Serita replaced the blindfold.

"So," Jade heard her say. "I will send men. Many men. Enjoy."

The door slammed shut and Jade knelt miserably. She had only a few minutes to wait however before the door opened again. Someone entered. A foot was pressed upon her neck, forcing it to the carpet. Jade found herself roughly handled. A hand passed over her wet sex. Then she wriggled as a cock pressed against her anus.

She served him blindly.

He was the first of many.

There was neither night nor day in that underground chamber. Jade did not know how long she served there and she lost count of the men who visited her. She did not see their faces. Always before they came, a valet entered the chamber and blindfolded her. Sometimes, he shortened the leash, forcing her to kneel with her cheek pressed against the rock. On each occasion she waited sightlessly, prepared and open, like a mare awaiting a stallion.

Her service was harsh. Often, they whipped her. Always, in some manner or other, they fucked her. At first, Jade was suitably horrified. Then, as her situation began to seem ever more surreal, she found herself revelling in the attention paid to her body. There was only sleep and sex for her there in that small chamber.

Eventually, there came the time when she was rudely wakened by the bite of a cane and a torch shone brightly in the darkness, causing her to shield her eyes as she lay upon the carpeted floor. The chain was unlocked from her collar.

"Out!"

It was the Head Valet's guttural voice. Jade painfully crawled to the low opening of the cell, out into the corridor.

"On your feet!"

She had not been upright for some time and her legs ached, but she somehow complied, and stood, hands on head, legs widely spread, regulation stance in the Dungeon.

"You have learned your lesson?"

"Yes, Master."

"No more trying to run away?"

"No, Master."

"Walk."

Jade stepped ahead of the Head Valet. Did this mean that the punishment was over?

She was escorted from the damp corridor, up a flight of stone steps, past the valets, outside into harsh daylight.

"Run. Knees up."

Strength returning to her legs, Jade obediently broke into a high-stepping, with the Head Valet jogging beside her. They passed groups of people - guests and slaves - who lay upon the manicured, watered lawns. Jade's breasts jiggled invitingly as she pranced past. Near the Round House, Serita stood waiting, barring their way, hands on hips.

"I take her."

"No!"

"It is the wish of the Host."

The Head Valet hesitated. "She has already been presented to the Host, before her escape." he said.

"I will present her again."

The man seemed as if about to brush Serita aside but then he turned aside. "Do as you will, then."

Serita smiled triumphantly as the Head Vale angrily strode way. She forced her fingers into the tight collar round Jade's neck, yanking her head back. To avoid being choked, the slave was obliged to stagger inelegantly backwards after the striding Serita.

Later, bathed and perfumed, her body lips smooth and freshly shaven,

Jade posed fearfully under the scrutiny of the Host. He briefly fingered the fiery stripes across her thighs and buttocks but made no comment.

"I have specially prepared her for you," Serita said, tapping Jade with a cane. She had been carefully rehearsed during those sessions in the Dungeon, and she knew what was required of her: obediently, she broke the pose, spread her legs widely, and bent double, the palms of her hands flat on the marble floor.

"Here," announced Serita, thrusting her fingers into the loosened bud of Jade's anus.

The Host frowned as he stooped to study the girl's puckered rose. "I hope she hasn't been damaged!"

"Not at all. The elastic is still there but she is opened for use - I do the same with the women Carlos keeps."

Jade squirmed as the Host gently thrust his finger into the orifice, which opened to admit the invading digit with surprising ease.

"It was too tight before," Serita explained, again tapping Jade's exposed buttocks.

Jade adjusted position, forcing her head between her spread thighs, below the nude nether lips.

"There!" Serita announced proudly. "You have her vagina, her arse is opened, and I have had her specially schooled in the art of oral sex. I call this the Unholy Trinity."

"Excellent!"

Serita turned to Jade. "You will strive to please the Host for me, little slut!"

"Yes, Mistress."

For Jade Preston, the torment, punishment and indignities suffered in the cold dark Dungeon had served their purpose. She was now utterly receptive to the demands made upon her and no longer even thought to protest. Serita Fernandez smiled triumphantly as she strode away across the lawn. The previously obdurate and proud Jade, her prodigy, would surrender abjectly. Serita had accomplished her task and scored points over the despised senior instructor. Soon, perhaps, she would be the Head Valet.

CHAPTER ELEVEN

Jade Clark fearfully reported for duty in the Conservatory: a cool, air-conditioned and shaded area where guests took their leisure during the day. Laced into a tight corset and clad in a scarlet gown of crackling taffeta, she was acutely conscious of bare breasts thrust upwards and rudely displayed. Moreover, the nipples had been rouged to match the deep scarlet of her gown. Talking was not allowed. Always, the slaves must conduct themselves with propriety, with eyes lowered, especially when in the Conservatory.

Almost immediately, a guest ordered that Jade be bent over a low footstool and her skirts were unceremoniously raised. The man's cock quickly penetrated her, and he roughly and vigorously took his pleasure. Afterwards, flushed and embarrassed, she sank quietly to her knees, carefully arranging the folds of the gown about her. That was how they wanted it.

She quickly learned to glance discretely from beneath lowered lashes, head still deferentially bowed. A cup required refilling here, a cigar needed lighting over there... each time, Jade would rise silently and move gracefully to attend the client. Her aim was to avoid further attention. Then the tip of her breast accidentally brushed the back of a guest's hand. She stepped back, blushing furiously. He laughed, grasping her wrist.

"You are new, aren't you?"

"Yes, Sir."

"Hitch up the front of your skirt."

Awkwardly, Jade stooped and carefully rolled up the material, securing it in the belt about her waist as the valets had taught her. The faille fabric fell away in diagonal folds to frame the blond triangle of her pubic hair. That is the way it was in the conservatory. Frequently, slaves were made to reveal themselves like that. Sometimes the skirts would be hitched up at the front, sometimes at the back and, on occasion, back and front at the same time.

The male slaves, though, were usually gloriously naked. They were shamelessly used, just like the women. Later that morning, Jade saw the German slave, Gunther, spread over a table, whipped, and then forced to take a cock in his backside. The women slaves looked on impassively and one woman was called upon to help. Her small hands delicately spread Gunther's buttocks, exposing the hairy puckered mouth there for the invasion. All of the slaves had to serve in the Conservatory at some time and in one way or another.

Jade was subtly different from the rest. Her shaven lips separated like the petals of a flower, revealing a large pink clitoris. It frequently drew attention when her skirt was hitched up, as on that morning.

"Ah!" one guest said, reaching to stroke Jade's silken flesh, "what have we here? It is always protruding strongly like this?"

"Sometimes," Jade stammered, utterly embarrassed.

"Often?"

"Quite often."

The man called a companion and they spent some time discussing her displayed charms in the crudest terms. One of the pair took hold of Jade from behind, his arm about her shoulders, fingers caressing her breasts and teasing her nipples.

Pulled backwards, off-balance, she was forced to spread her legs and thrust forward her hips to meet the expert caresses administered by the other man. Without haste, the man before her unfastened his clothing to free a large, erect organ. His accomplice thrust a knee into the small of her back, forcing her pelvis forward to invite ravishment.

The wet, welcoming flesh of her femininity opened to accept the man's strong thrusts. Sally and the other women, their skirts hitched high and breasts bare, looked on. When the first was done, the men reversed roles and Jade was held stooped as the second took her from the rear, giving out little gasps of exertion as he insinuated his cock into her puckered bud. As Jade had been specially prepared there, she took the organ without difficulty.

Afterwards, acutely aware of the other slaves who impassively watched her humiliation, Jade knelt shyly before the two guests and carefully fastened their clothing with trembling fingers. The training room, no matter how arduous and explicit the instruction, could never really compare with this.

Jade, it appeared, received harsher attention in the training room than the others. Was it just because of her monumental disobedience in trying to escape? Or was it because of her thrusting and abnormally large clitoris?

Thrusting her pelvis forward as demanded, she further revealed the pink bud which burst from her body lips. To her surprise, Jade now viewed it as a redeeming feature. In this place, the protruding nubbin was the subject of wondering admiration. The Head Valet and his assistants frequently referred to it.

Also, of course, the clitoris was her point of vulnerability and weakness. They occasionally gave it a playful tweak, particularly after punishment, when it was hard and engorged; she dared not protest or try to avoid the teasing fingers. Instead, blushingly open, she surrendered to their attentions. It was utterly degrading and yet her body was quickly inflamed. Her male colleagues in bondage would look on. She did not care about their witnessing her humiliation for they were only slaves like her, and she frequently saw them subjected to similar degradations.

"Repeat after me," the trainer called, "'I love myself in my slavery.'"

"I love myself in my slavery," each of the group intoned. "I love myself in my slavery."

"I free myself to be a slave."

"I free myself to be a slave," Jade said, looking at her own image in the glass. "I love my body and am not ashamed."

Even as she gazed into the mirror a familiar ache was beginning to throb in her vagina and it was becoming wet. At this point, quite against her will, she always experienced the same moist warmth spreading from the pit of her belly. Jade took a deep breath and slowly began to caress her own body. She flaunted her gradual arousal, knowing that people were probably watching on the other side of the mirror.

The men always climaxed first, large cocks grasped in their hands, spouting gushes of semen. Jade was usually the first woman to bring herself to orgasm. She even secretly thrilled in the unavoidable exhibitionism. The very smell of the training room at such times excited her. Perhaps the Host and Serita had been right and she was nothing more than a wanton slut. In any event, Jade's stifled moans of release soon echoed around the room.

Panting and warm she watched the other women in fascination. Before her abduction, Jade had never seen either a man or a woman masturbating. This daily session of self-love was supposed to be a kindness. The training sessions were designed to arouse them. Ritual self-love, then, was a release from the frustrations of pent-up sexuality - a natural and calculated climax of their training session. At no other time were they allowed to touch themselves. Even at night, temptation was removed by the tethering of their hands to their collars.

Presently they all stood panting in the training room, their bodies flushed. Suddenly coy, Jade averted her eyes from the mirror.

"She is quite lovely even now," said the tall, distinguished man who critically viewed Jade from the other side of the glass.

"Yes, Sir," the Head Valet replied. "but the Host is particularly interested in this one."

"I will examine her when she has been showered."

"To the showers."

The slaves sped off to the steam-filled shower-room. Sebastian somehow insinuated himself to Jade's side under the gushing shower heads.

"How are you bearing up?" he whispered, his hand illicitly smoothing the soapy lather upon her breast.

"Fine. You?"

"Okay, I guess. More than that. I love it here."

Jade looked up in surprise and she saw that he was smiling. "Is there someone you love here then?" she asked, aware that Sebastian had been used sexually by many men and women guests.

"No," he said. "I don't love anyone. I love the life and the punishments. Does that offend you?"

Jade was aware that a valet was nearby, ready to whip them for daring to speak with each other.

"Yes," she told Sebastian before moving away. "I think you are quite mad and utterly debauched."

Yet, even as she spoke, visibly wounding Sebastian, Jade knew that she was also becoming ensnared by the sexuality of her slavery. She cast another glance at him from beneath lowered eyelashes, and then at other male slaves. Their hard bodies were glistening under the water, shrouded in steam. Even when flaccid, their cocks held a fascination for her. Forcing these thoughts away, she hurriedly finished her shower.

"Jade!" the Head Valet called.

"Yes, Sir?"

"To the surgery. As you are. Run!"

She looked up in surprise but was quick enough to avoid his swishing whip, running along the corridor and out into the hot sunshine. Everything was always at the double: rush here, run there. Jade found it terribly degrading to be run, breasts bouncing, before guests and other servants, but her body was certainly fitter than when she had arrived on the island and she reached the surgery some feet ahead of the trotting man.

Jade was ushered before a tall, distinguished looking stranger who waited in the surgery. He looked at her heaving bosom and frowned. "A women's breasts should be provided with support when subjected to vigorous exercise," he said disapprovingly. "Step forward, girl."

Jade flinched as the man's cold slender hands delicately cupped her breasts. He lifted first one and then the other, allowing them to drop to judge their firmness, squeezed each fleshy orb and then roughly measured the position of her nipples, using splayed finger and thumb. Then he made her lie on an examination couch and she silently submitted to his handling.

The Doctor had conducted a similar exploration on her arrival, but this man seemed more practised and firm. She was ordered to kneel up on the couch, on all fours, as he stooped to eye the pendent fall of her breasts.

"What do you think?" asked the Head Valet.

"Yes," the man replied slowly, "there is scope for some augmentation and reshaping. We will what we can."

Horrified, Jade started at the man's words. "May I speak?" she blurted.

"Silence!" barked the Head Valet.

"But -" Her words tailed off with a scream as his whip seared across her raised buttocks.

Jade sobbed but otherwise remained silent for the remainder of the ordeal. Her body was pummelled, pinched and prodded. The man was not gentle. She was made to lie on her back, legs draped over the sides of the couch to widely splay her thighs. On command, she held the denuded sex lips apart to fully reveal her jutting clitoris. She closed her eyes to shut out the humiliation but jumped involuntarily when his thumb and forefinger delicately gripped and tugged at the sensitive nub.

"You are absolutely sure about this?"

"Instructions of the Host."

"Well, it won't be a problem. As for the rest... a nose bob, some tucks here and there... I'll need photographs. What is her name?"

"Preston. Mrs Jade Preston."

John Preston was not in the best of moods when he left the foyer of the plush Hilton Hotel in Istanbul. He did not know why, for the business transaction was going particularly well. His meeting that morning had been smooth enough, and the deal was certainly going to be profitable. It was just that something kept nagging at his mind... this deal, the biggest of his career, was too pat, too easy. Innate suspicion again, that was all. Why could he not simply accept it and just enjoy himself?

There had been plenty of enjoyment!

In addition to the resident ministrations of Leila and Rachel, a steady stream of suppliant and beautiful women seemed to flow to his door nowadays. Long leisure hours had been filled with heady, erotic delights.

When Preston emerged from the building that morning, Leila dutifully waited, as always, in the plush car; the woman was never late. She held a peeled grape between her tiny, perfect teeth and, as Preston sat beside her - he had long since abandoned the practice of sitting in the rear - she pressed the grape to his lips, forcing it into his mouth with her tongue.

"Am I supposed to be impressed?"

"The peeled grape is a time-honoured way for a slave girl to beg for love," the young woman said with a smile as she smoothly eased her vehicle into the hectic stream of Istanbul's midday traffic. "In the seraglio she will peel the grapes, one by one, all the time dreaming of her handsome master. At night she feeds them to him with her teeth until he can no longer resist her."

"I see."

"Sometimes, a girl will masturbate while she peels the grapes so that her love scent will arouse her handsome master as he takes each grape."

"You did that?"

"Are you aroused?" Leila asked with a provocative flash of her eyes.

Preston did not reply. Normally, he delighted in her games and his lack of interest that day was something of an aberration. In fact, Preston realised that he was becoming besotted with the artful little Armenian. Rachel, too, in a way - but with Leila it was different. Her playful and seductive manner completely enchanted him and she had quickly made him forget his sadness at the loss of Jade.

Leila was sexually insatiable. Continuously innovative, the Armenian usually invented the erotic tales with which she enticed him, and her story about the grapes was probably another example. Had she really fed him a grape smeared with her love juices?

"I am hungry for you," Leila pouted as she manoeuvred the car through the busy city centre. "What must I do today to excite my Master?"

Tantalisingly, she began to unbutton her short coat. It swung open to reveal her magnificent breasts, gold rings piercing the nipples. She had long since realised that these aroused him to almost uncontrollable excitement. With an artful sideways look as she drove through the city centre, Leila began to toy provocatively with one of the rings.

"Cover yourself. You'll get us both arrested."

"Then you must beat me for disobedience," she laughed.

Oblivious to the astonished stares from lascivious but mainly repressed Turks, the unashamed and bare-breasted Leila drove slowly through the traffic. Preston's handsome features glowered with anger but he relaxed somewhat once safely clear of the city centre.

When they arrived home, Leila took his briefcase and preceded him into the villa. Slipping off the coat and posing prettily, she meaningfully caressed her crotch and gestured towards a silver tray laden with peeled grapes.

"She is to be beaten," Preston told Rachel grimly. "Fix me a drink and then tie her in the courtyard."

Rachel smiled. Preston knew that this beautiful creature had only reluctantly accepted her place as second woman in the household. Oh, she continued to present herself attractively, and Preston frequently used her. Sometimes the three of them cavorted together. It was different with Leila, however: the little minx had captivated Preston and she enjoyed a privileged status.

Thus, it was usually Rachel who squirmed beneath his lash in punishment while, with a flutter of long black eye-lashes, the artful Armenian could usually avoid a beating.

Rachel handed a tumbler of iced whisky to Preston and then, taking hold of one of Leila's nipple rings, she led the pouting girl from the room.

Preston was still very angry. In his line of business he could not afford unwarranted attention. Turkey is a Moslem country and its judges are harsh with those who outrage its moral codes. Leila's behaviour could have resulted in serious problems and Turkish gaols are not pleasant. Besides, she had wilfully disobeyed his order.

When he walked into the courtyard an hour later, he found Leila completely naked and securely tied. She whimpered in protest: "Rachel is a bitch to tie me like this."

Preston smiled grimly. The girl's position was indeed uncomfortable. She leaned forward, doubled over the stone balustrade, her hands secured around one of the wide pillars which supported the pantile roof of the veranda. Worse, a chain attached to her nipple rings tightly encircled the pillar, requiring that she compress her chest against the cool marble.

Leila clasped the pillar to her breasts as if adoring a huge phallus. Her back was necessarily arched and she stood on the tips of her toes, presenting tight, uplifted buttocks for punishment. She adjusted her position slightly to ease the ache in her limbs but the tie permitted little movement. She groaned as Preston took the belt that Rachel had thoughtfully placed within Leila's vision on the balustrade rail.

The painfully bound woman tensed with expectation as Preston moved behind her. He stung her with an exploratory flick of the belt, catching her bottom with its swishing tip and causing her to squeal and flinch involuntarily. He flicked the belt upon her body a number of times over the next few minutes. Each time the body leapt but, as Preston intended, she learned to control her movements and ease the pressure on her breasts; he did not want her to tear the tender flesh. Satisfied that she could keep her upper body relatively motionless, he stood back and raised the broad belt high. It whistled through the air and seared agonising pain across Leila's upraised, tense buttocks.

She screamed.

After the stinging torment of tiny flicks, she was surprised by the suddenness and severity of the blow. Although she danced on the tips of her toes, her tethered breasts remained hugged to the pillar. Preston insisted that she adjust her position, raising herself to the very points of her toes, legs straight and taut, her back greatly arched and buttocks thrust back. He then delivered the second blow, laying it across the first.

Again she screamed and jigged frantically, waddling her bottom as if it were on fire. He was patient, waiting, keeping her tensed with fearful anticipation. The third cut swept upwards, into the slight crease at the lower swell of her buttocks, and Leila's toes left the ground as she leapt upward.

And so it continued. Leila's punishment was severe. From time to time, Preston stopped to inspect her nipples but, although thrusting, erect and very reddened, they remained undamaged by the tight chain. Then the beating continued, slowly and deliberately, calculated for maximum mental and physical effect. Leila, thoroughly chastised, gave a grateful gasp when he eventually replaced the bet on the balustrade rail. She closed her eyes and pressed her tear-stained cheek against the marble of the pillar.

"A girl is sorry," she sobbed. "Oh, oh!"

Her penetration was sudden and fierce. Regardless of the scorching pain, Leila joyfully began to grind her hips to meet her master's rhythmic thrusts.

Later, John Preston sipped iced whisky and watched with mild interest as Leila lay upon her belly while Rachel applied a soothing unguent to the fiery flesh.

"It is as well," Rachel told her. "The organisation will see that we have taught him to be strong. Anyway, you have something to remember him by when you leave tomorrow."

Preston started forward in surprise. "Leave? You are leaving tomorrow?"

Leila turned her head towards him and smiled sadly. "I have been re-called. I was going to tell you after you had indulged in my peeled grapes."

"You can't leave. I forbid it!"

"There are masters who are even stronger than you, John Preston," Leila said.

When Jade Preston regained consciousness in the hospital block, she was not at first aware of any pain. Discomfort, yes, but not pain. The effect of the numbing and befuddling drugs gradually wore off, however, and then the soreness became almost too much to bear.

With the return of rational thought, she experienced a mixture of fury, utter dejection and fear: they had treated her like an animal with no control over her own destiny or, even, over her own body. She did not know what had been done to her, only that it was without any consultation or permission.

Her wrists, waist and ankles were strapped securely. Unable to move, she could not decide which part of her body hurt more. She could actually see the puffy, swollen cheeks of her face and a distracting mass of flesh-coloured sticking plaster over her nose. Any movement of facial muscles, particularly the nostrils, caused acute discomfort. She could tell that her breasts were heavily bandaged and they were very sore.

Jade heard herself scream.

"Shut up, stupid woman," the nurse scolded as she hurried into the room.

"Please untie me."

"Later." The white-smocked nurse was calmly preparing a syringe. "Just relax."

"You had no right..."

The nurse administered the injection and, only moments later, Jade lapsed into semi-consciousness and no longer cared what had been done to her.

Further operations followed. Over a period of weeks, Jade Preston was gradually transformed in accordance with the Host's detailed specification. Fat was removed from her hips and belly, the sacs beneath her eyes were reduced.

As the pain, swelling and scars faded, Jade was able to see the startling effect each time she looked in a mirror. Strict diet and regular, enforced exercise supplemented the surgeon's expertise.

The trainers were keen to reinforce the reality of Jade's new, lowly station upon her psyche. They regularly exercised her sexual urges and she had little say in the matter but, then, neither did she want a choice. Thus a stream of men - guests, valets and even male slaves - visited her quarters in the Medical Block. She never knew when to expect them, or how many there would be.

Sebastian was ordered to her once and he took her brutally and without pity, perhaps still smarting from her disparaging remarks in the showers. Initially, Jade was only alerted to impending use each time valets chained her wrists to the bed-head. After a while, however, as she became more suppliant, they did not always do that.

Jade complied with the rapacious demands, mindful of the real threat of punishment. Anyway, the needs of her body quickly took over. She not only submitted to each visitor but wantonly abandoned herself to the pleasure. Before the scars healed, they had to tie her down for her own good. The bondage further inflamed her and she became a bucking and grunting she-cat in heat, begging for more. When Sebastian was again brought to her, she fucked with a voracious ardour and he laughed unkindly at her wantonness.

"You, too, Jade," he had said, and she knew just what he meant.

Later, to avoid possible damage to the new breasts, they tied her face-down over a padded table, with buttocks upraised. Once they sent three men, one after the other, and she never saw their faces, or knew who they were, just as in that red-carpeted chamber.

When the bandages had been removed and her bruises were healing, the Host paid a visit. Jade remained silent, prodded, twisted and turned, as he inspected her like a prize heifer. His delight was apparent. Afterwards, he satiated his lust upon her and he was surprisingly gentle, almost respectful.

"Excellent, my dear," he said afterwards. "You are ready for Big Hall, I think."

When the Host returned to his office, the Head Valet awaited him there.

"The girl has arrived from Istanbul," he said.

"I will see her."

Minutes later, Leila entered. She was utterly naked, except for her erotic nipple rings and a green collar locked upon her slender neck. She clasped her hands behind her neck, thrusting out her breasts. Her legs were widely spread.

The Host rose from his chair and circled her. He stooped as he casually examined the fiery marks on her olive-hued skin.

"John Preston beat you?"

"Yes, Sir. I was punished for disobedience."

"Excellent! Now, tell me all about him. What are his likes and dislikes? I want a full report. What in a woman particularly excites him?"

Leila licked her lips as she considered the question, fingering the ring that pierced her right nipple.

CHAPTER TWELVE

"Ready for Big Hall," the valet called.

A dozen or more women and, perhaps, half a dozen men, immediately rose from the sunken pool where they had spent a pleasant hour in warm, perfumed water.

Since being exhibited there, Jade had not visited Big Hall. She sat quietly as a woman expertly coiffured her hair and then, naked, she padded into a large dressing room. The other women were left to prepare themselves with minimal supervision. Some were already dressing as a valet guided Jade to a vacant seat. The low stool was covered with a prickly fur which tickled her flesh as she sat. She applied make-up to her face and the valet insisted that she make a slight amendment before nodding his approval.

"You are privileged tonight," the Head Valet told her as she sat there naked and apprehensive. "You may speak and dine with the guests. It will not always be so."

They had allowed her to dress.

A small corset, little more than a wide belt, was cinched tightly about her waist. Sheer stockings, nothing more: Jade accepted that normal lingerie was from now on forbidden to her, that she must go naked beneath any clothing they deigned to allow. Licking her glistening lips with anticipation, she slipped into an elegant and surprisingly demure white gown.

The first guests were arriving in Big Hall. Slaves allotted to serving duties were already at work. Waitresses stood ready in black and white tunics - any impression of primness quickly dispelled by a flash of bare buttock beneath their incredibly short skirts as they walked. Wine waitresses were clad in gauze drapes which tantalisingly revealed the naked promise beneath. Male slaves, nude, cocks and balls harnessed, served too. Some females, those who tended the cloak room, those performing reception and escort duties, and croupiers at the gaming tables, wore deeply plunging gowns, cut to leave breasts and sex wholly exposed.

The clients may have been select - chosen for wealth, discretion and perverse tastes - but Jade saw that they were plentiful enough. It seemed that this resort was immensely attractive with its supply of young and compliant men and women, their health and discretion guaranteed.

Jade stayed shyly in the background, wondering at the splendour of Big Hall. Elegantly dressed and stunningly undressed, beautiful women wandered its vastness. These trained slaves, delicious all, paraded the room as whores, fully and helplessly available to any of the guests who wanted them. The men, too, Sebastian among them, unashamedly displayed their muscles and strong cocks. Big Hall was a vast temple dedicated to erotic pleasure.

"Ah, there you are," Serita said, taking Jade by the elbow. "I have someone who wants to meet you. You will be very nice to him!"

The Spanish beauty ushered Jade to a table where three middle-aged men sat with two stunning young women known to Jade from the training rooms. One of the men immediately rose and gallantly held a chair.

"You must be Jade. This is your first time in Big Hall?"

"Yes."

"Then it is my great honour and responsibility."

The others laughed and Jade smiled uncertainly. An orchestra played discrete background music as guests mingled and engaged in sophisticated small-talk. Wine waitresses, their beauty ill-concealed, wandered from table to table. Most of the enslaved women wore green collars, although a few, like Jade, wore red ones. Although the collared women affected easy gaiety, Jade thought that there was a strained air to it all; the free women, on the other hand, seemed to revel in their superiority. Jade craved a sip of wine but she knew that alcohol was forbidden to her.

The evening progressed pleasantly enough. It was an excellent meal - Jade delighted in the opportunity to eat luxuriously after the regime of fruit and gruel. The men chatted amiably and they were the epitome of propriety in their behaviour towards the girls. When the orchestra struck up, John invited Jade to dance with him and she almost began to forget her place in the order of things.

"All is well?" Serita asked as she approached the group. "You are enjoying the evening and ready for the entertainment?"

"Certainly," John replied.

A fanfare of trumpets. The house-lights dimmed. Jade started forward in surprise as spotlights suddenly beamed upon her. Serita hissed an order into her ear and, commanded, Jade rose nervously to her feet, aware of the eyes upon her. Across the room, another girl, wearing a green collar, also stood in the beam of a spotlight. John rose to his feet and, taking Jade's arm, escorted her to the centre of the floor. Smiling encouragingly, he left her there with the green-collar girl.

"Ladies and gentlemen, this evening is a special occasion for those two ladies. This is their first appearance in Big Hall. Jade and Sally will now remove their clothing."

Jade gasped. Sally, however, shrugged resignedly and reached back to unzip her tight black dress, quickly removing the garment and standing naked but for dark stockings and high heeled shoes. Jade hesitated. Although now accustomed to being nude before others, she had never been forced to undress in these circumstances. It seemed that they had provided her with clothing merely for the exquisite humiliation of taking it from her.

"Strip, you little fool," Serita's voice whispered urgently from outside the spotlight. "Or you will be severely beaten!"

Defeated, Jade pulled down the bodice of the demure white dress. After a moment's hesitation she tugged the tight material over her hips and allowed it to fall to the floor before stepping awkwardly from the discarded gown. Both women wore small garter corsets, stockings and high, stiletto-heeled shoes, nothing more. Jade's highly-slit mound was denuded and fully revealed, while the other girl's sex was clothed in a neat triangle of fair curly hair.

"Posture!"

The command was familiar. Both women immediately assumed a provocative pose, with hips turned.

"Walk!"

The two stripped slaves perambulated the length of the dance floor before returning to pose at its centre. It was perhaps harder for Jade, an unpleasant surprise, whereas Sally seemed to have known what to expect.

"Strip completely," Serita ordered.

Head bowed, Jade removed the last scanty items from her body. When both slaves were utterly naked, the music commenced, raw and demanding.

"Dance, sluts!" Serita commanded.

Sally immediately began to move with the beat, and she heard Jade screech, whipped. There was no choice, both knew that. Jade, too, began to move with the music. The dance movements, so frequently practised in the training room, were deliberately provocative and designed to display the dancers as erotically as possible.

Jade danced well now, as she must. The two women swirled around the floor as the audience clapped in time to the insistent beat.

Suddenly, it was over. They stood, breasts heaving, in a stylised pose. A man came to offer his arm to Jade. She took it shyly, blushing furiously, her head bowed. The guest escorted her back to the table, warmly applauded by other guests. Nude, embarrassed and awkward, breathing heavily and wiping perspiration from her brow, Jade sat upon the leather chair, feeling the slick hide stick to her thighs. Another man stepped forward and caressed Sally's breasts. She smiled and accompanied him prettily from the floor.

Later, in the privacy of a luxury chalet, Sally performed fully and energetically; her escort was not dissatisfied with his prize. Elsewhere, in another chalet with another guest, Jade Preston was performing also. Discipline was strict and slaves have little choice but, secretly, both Sally and Jade found themselves glorying in their slavery.

After her unnerving introduction in Big Hall, Jade was much sought-after by the guests. The weeks had brought about a remarkable change in her. All reserve gone, she had become a sensuous, lascivious creature without inhibition or, it seemed, shame.

That she had little choice in the matter was a prime factor in her eager submission: valets simply delivered her to those guests who wanted her, and this gave her a perverse thrill. Like the other slaves, Jade was punished if found less than pleasing but, in truth, she eagerly participated in her ravishment. Such was the change in Jade Preston. Perhaps she was one of those people who only find true sexual freedom when in abject slavery.

She had become accustomed to routine degradation and humiliation but she always had a delicious dread of training under the instruction of her mistress, Serita Fernandez. Although the woman was extremely harsh with all the girls, she seemed to delight specially in inflicting the most humiliating ordeals upon Jade.

"Lick, Jade. With the tip of your tongue," Serita demanded in the training room. "That's it, little slut, caress its length. Not so vigorously - he will come too quickly. Gently. Make it last. Turn and straddle him with your pussy hovering over his mouth. Keep licking. That's it. Trail your nipples over his chest. No, keep your cunt up, you little slut."

"Yes, Mistress," Jade called as the tip of Serita's cane tapped her bottom.

The man, a strapping blond German, one of the handsome male slaves, lay supine on the floor as Jade artfully wriggled her bottom above his face, knowing how he would have loved to lick at her naked slit. She also knew that he dare not move until Serita allowed it, so she teasingly danced her long tumescent clitoris before his eyes. Jade was becoming quite skilled under the tutelage of the ever-demanding Serita.

"Natasha, straddle him but do not take him in."

Natasha shuddered visibly. She spread her legs on either side of the man's body and then squatted down near Jade's bobbing head. The erect, glistening member just touched Natasha's moist sex lips, exciting her exposed bud. Jade continued her task, her hair tickling the Russian's shaven love mound.

"Down, Natasha."

Natasha, carefully balanced, with knees flexed either side of Jade's bobbing head, began to lower herself onto the rampant organ. Gunther groaned with delight.

Serita watched Jade critically as her splayed thighs straddled the young man's face, and she smiled as the slave threw back her head as Gunther's tongue invaded her sex. At the same time, Natasha surrendered to her own desires and she wildly rode out the lust of the impressively erect male slave.

"Not yet!" Jade yelled.

Gunther abandoned all self-discipline and hungrily lapped at Jade's vagina. Both women were fully aroused and the groans and scents of sex filled the air. Presently, the German let out a muffled roar and this was closely followed by an anguished screech from Natasha, who furiously pumped her body up and down on the ejaculating penis within her. Jade, giving desperate little moans, continued to grind her womanhood into the man's face.

"Jade! Enough!" Serita shouted. "Do you want to suffocate him?"

"Mistress!" Jade protested, still hungry for satisfaction.

A sharp swish of the cane stilled her. Jade sullenly climbed from the exhausted but smiling Gunther. She glared at Natasha, who hung her head, shamed. She had been so quick! Jade brushed the hair from her face and looked down sullenly as the male slave, satiated, scrambled to his feet and grinned broadly.

"Thank him," Serita commanded.

"Mistress," Jade protested. "He is only a slave."

"Thank him."

"Thank you, Gunther," Jade said grudgingly.

"Natasha."

"Thank you, Gunther."

"As for you Jade," Serita said, "that will be six stripes. If you are slow in learning obedience, then I don't mind."

"Mistress!"

"Ten strokes."

Gunther smiled at Jade's outrage, and Natasha turned away to gaze into the training mirror. Serita forced Jade to lie on the floor, face up, legs doubled over so that her toes touched on either side of her head. Then the Spanish woman went behind, seized her victim's ankles and crossed them behind her neck. Jade's back was bowed and her naked buttocks separated to reveal the puckered rose there. Her splayed thighs and opened sex were presented upturned, awaiting Serita's cane.

"Ready? Ten! Count them off. Begin."

"One!" Jade called in a tremulous voice, and the first measured blow scorched across the very top of her thighs, even stinging the moist, glistening lips of her exposed vulva. She screeched but remained in position.

"Two," Jade counted, tensing her buttocks.

When the punishment was over, the slave, thoroughly chastened, rose to her feet.

"You must now report to the Doctor," Serita said. She added: "It is the Host's orders."

Jade nodded and, after hastily showering, she hurried over to the Medical Block.

"Lie on the bed," the nurse instructed, leaving Jade naked in a small anteroom.

Jade's modesty had been compromised long since and she was little concerned by nudity nowadays. The nurse reappeared, carrying a stainless steel tray which she carefully laid upon a nearby table. Jade meekly allowed the woman to strap broad leather belts about her chest and belly. Then her wrists and ankles were secured to the corners of the bed and she lay spread-eagled, quite unable to move. The nurse busied herself at the table, arranging a number of medical instruments.

After some minutes the Doctor entered. He tested the straps. No explanation was given as he prepared a hypodermic syringe.

Frightened now, Jade tried to protest, but in vain.

The doctor injected first one breast and then the other. Then, taking a numbed nipple between finger and thumb, he quickly clamped a stainless steel instrument about the distended flesh. She heard a metallic click and, despite the anaesthetic, felt a sharp stinging pain, then a small gold rod was threaded into the hole which pierced her flesh.

Looking down in horror, Jade realised what had been done and she heard herself scream. The straps held her secure as she attempted to writhe, not in pain but in anguish. Then the Doctor calmly repeated the process on her other nipple.

Still he was not finished. Local anaesthetic was applied to her opened feminine intimacies. Jade, held prone on the bed, could not see what he was doing but she could feel the strange sensation of fingers probing her numbed flesh. And another sharp piercing sensation, this time at the very seat of her womanhood.

He similarly treated her navel. There was nothing she could do to prevent it.

The remainder of the treatment was relatively straightforward: The Doctor quickly pierced her ears and the septum of her nose, each time inserting small rods to prevent the holes from healing together. Later, the small rods were removed, and golden rings were welded in their place.

"Now," the Head Valet said, "look at little Jade. Isn't she beautiful?"

It was the first time that she had rejoined her companions for many days. She stood winsomely naked in front of the mirror. The creature who stared back was indeed beautiful but strangely barbaric. Large golden bangles hung from her ears and a small fine band pierced the septum of her nose. And more, golden rings now hung from her thick nipples and the pierced flesh of her navel was similarly adorned.

Her large clitoris seemed even more pronounced: a gleaming band of gold now pierced the erotic nub. It lay flat against the surrounding tissue, hiding within her labia, but the band was of sufficient diameter and weight to push the lips slightly apart from the thrusting member.

Her sensitivity was even further enhanced, and the merest manipulation of the metal link on her clitoris, even tiny vibrating taps, sent spasms coursing through her loins. The natural movement of her body as she walked slightly agitated the ring and seemed to keep the clitoris constantly erect. Her subjugation was utter and complete now. Those seven light golden rings that pierced her secured Jade Preston in bondage as surely as any iron chain.

She did not flinch when the Head Valet knelt to part her beauty lips, fully revealing the gleaming, glistening golden ring. Natasha gasped audibly at the sight.

"The Host commands your company tonight," the Head Valet said, reaching into the pocket of his red waistcoat and producing a small silver bell. "For his pleasure, you must have another ornament."

Jade's heart palpitated. The Host! But then, she thought, it is to be expected that he should wish to be the first to use her in her newly-pierced state. There was little time for more thoughts, however, for the Head Valet was reaching between her beauty lips to grasp the ring that pierced her sensitised clitoris. He twisted the ring forward so that it forced her nether lips to remain apart and he then clipped the bell in place. It hung slightly forward, beneath the tip of the unusual nubbin. Similar bells were then attached to her nipples.

"Walk," he commanded.

Blushing hotly, Jade walked around the perimeter of the training room. The bell between her legs was surprisingly heavy and it tinkled with each sway of her body. She could not avoid seeing the vision of her own barbaric adornment emphasising her nudity in the mirrors.

Now, with the bell, everyone would know what had been done to her. But, amid these thoughts, was a dreadful and excited anticipation at the prospect of serving the Host again.

Jade walked smartly across the gardens, sometimes almost running behind the valet who strode along in front. He held a leash that was attached to the ring at her clitoris, and she was anxious to avoid any pressure there. After being bathed and perfumed, she had fully expected the feathered mask to be locked upon her, blotting out all hearing and sight. But no, she was to be delivered utterly naked. Being nude among clothed people was a normal if still humiliating state for her now.

The valet led her through the thronged foyer of Big Hall, and up the stairs to the plushly carpeted corridors above.

"Hands and knees!"

Jade obediently dropped down, feeling the tight leash droop from her loins as it was released by the man. Kneeling on all fours, looking down past her pendent breasts with their barbaric rings and bells, she saw the valet's hand reach between her spread legs to take the trailing leash. As he pulled it taut, Jade felt the thin strap cleave between her buttocks.

"Forward!"

A little tug on the leash urged her on, and she crawled at almost a trot towards the double doors that fronted the Host's quarters. She obediently knelt up to reach the ornate brass handles and push the doors open. Another tug at her womanhood, painful this time, and Jade crawled gasping into the room beyond.

Serita lolled on a white leather chaise longue, watching indolently as Jade crawled forward. The Spanish woman was beautifully radiant in a full length evening gown that moulded to every curve of her body, and her long mane of black glossy hair draped forward over her shoulder as she lay propped upon one elbow.

The valet guided Jade to the very side of the sofa.

"Kneel up, little slut," Serita said, "Let me see your adornments."

Jade obeyed instantly and, without instruction, she placed her hands behind her neck and thrust out her belled breasts. Serita reached forward to hold one of the little brass bells, shaking it to hear its crystal sound. Then her fingers gently traced the nipple, where the golden ring entered the flesh; she slowly pushed the tight button first one way, then the other, scratching with a long pointed finger nail at the soft honey-coloured flesh surrounding it.

Jade looked straight ahead, breathing evenly, as the woman handled her. She parted her legs wider, an involuntary act, when Serita reached to tug at the leash, to part her beauty lips, and to tickle the clitoris there.

What had happened to her? She felt Serita's cool fingers toying with her secret parts. How could she be kneeling naked and enslaved, inspected like a pet dog by this clothed and haughty woman? Serita frightened her, more than any of the other trainers or valets, more than the Host himself. It was a fear, she knew, borne of a forbidden excitement that she felt whenever this woman tormented and humiliated her.

Then, quite suddenly, Serita slapped Jade's breasts with such force that she cried out. This spurred the woman to smack her there again, once, twice, three times more. The soft flesh burned and ached, causing tears to stream down Jade's face.

"Kiss your master's feet," Serita ordered, turning her head away imperiously.

The Host, who had watched with interest, rose and stood waiting. The valet pulled on the leash, giving the merest twitch to the now throbbing clitoris, and Jade wept softly as, hands still clasped at her neck, she stooped to kiss the Host's polished shoes.

"You must be very firm with her," Jade heard Serita say. "It is a kindness in the long run."

"She is coming along quite nicely," the Host said. "She is a natural slave."

Jade almost gagged at his words. They seemed to know her so well. Then, to her astonishment, she heard Serita laugh.

"You say that because you are besotted with the little slut."

Besotted? Could this be true? But Serita ordered her up once more. There was no time to think any more, and perhaps it was best not to, anyway. Again, Jade winced as her breasts were slapped spitefully from side to side. Serita reached upwards to stroke the tear-streaked cheeks, tracing a manicured and painted fingernail over the quivering lips and touching the lowered eyelids. Jade shivered, and the clasp of her fingers tightened behind her neck.

"I see why the Host is besotted by you, little slut," she murmured, half to herself.

"Bring her to the bedroom," the Host instructed, himself strolling towards the door. "You may examine her at your leisure there."

Serita roused herself from the sofa and, taking the leash, she dismissed the valet with a gesture of her head. Then, pushing Jade forward by the shoulders onto all fours, she spitefully jerked upon the tether to send a delicious pain shooting upwards through her pelvis.

Jade crawled forward, following the Host. He was standing beside a large chest of drawers, delving inside an opened drawer, when she entered the bedroom. Even as she crawled forward, Jade saw the ornate feathered mask lying upon the black silk sheet upon the bed.

"Have her stand," the Host said casually, taking a flat paddle shaped object from the drawer.

Jade climbed to her feet, blanching as the Host swished the supple leather paddle through the air. She spread her feet widely and clenched her buttocks as Serita unclipped the cruel leash.

"Relax," Serita said, stroking the silky cheeks. "And fold your arms behind you, flat against your back."

This was a new and uncomfortable imposition, but Jade struggled to obey. The position thrust her breasts forward with even more prominence.

"Brace yourself," the Host said. "The blows of this paddle will be quite strong and you must not move."

Jade caught her breath in a sob. She wanted to break position and run.

"Come now," he said, noticing the tiny moan. "You want to give me pleasure, do you not?"

"Yes Master," Jade murmured, adjusting her arms and thrusting out her breasts.

"Then save your whimpering for when the paddle begins to smart."

Jade bit her quivering lip and consciously stiffened, trying at the same time to relax her buttocks as Serita had demanded. She swayed in shock as the paddle smacked loudly against her soft flesh. The next blow was even harder, and an incredible wave of sharp pain exploded on her furiously hot bottom. His third and fourth blows followed swiftly, giving Jade no time to recover and she yelped loudly.

The Host came to the front and tenderly caressed her face, cradling her chin in his hands and wiping tears away with his thumbs. "That wasn't so bad, was it?" he intoned.

"No," Jade lied, her buttocks afire. "Why have I been beaten?"

"Because it pleases me. I want to release your body to be a true slave. When you are beaten, you must think only of that. And rejoice that it is being done to you."

But how? Jade thought. Could he know how much it hurt her? Yet he bent her over and began to spank her anew, cracking the paddle against her flaming bottom with a steady rhythm. Finally, he stopped.

"That will do for now," he said, breathing heavily. "Come, lie on the bed."

Jade did as she was bid, lying on her back before gingerly lowering her stinging buttocks onto the cool silk sheets. Her legs were spread, and the upraised position of her sore buttocks presented the shaven sex for his eyes.

Yet it was Serita, and not the Host, who climbed beside her. The woman had pulled down the top of her black slinky gown to reveal small firm breasts tipped with the darkest maroon. She looked down at Jade, licking her lips salaciously, as her hand trailed over the slave's taut belly.

Jade began to breathe more quickly now, particularly as the woman's cool fingers parted her sex lips. She felt so wet there and there was a familiar, dull ache in her vagina.

"Spread your legs wider."

Jade opened her legs further.

"I said wider!" Serita rasped, smacking the soft inner flesh of Jade's thighs until the tormented young woman's knees were splayed and pressing against the silk sheets.

Jade closed her eyes and thought of the supreme ignominy of her status. Where was the pampered and sophisticated middle class woman now, she thought, as she felt Serita's thumbs enter and wrench open her vagina. She was profoundly humiliated and wanted to flee back to her safe life in London. That, of course, was impossible now. Would it ever be possible again? Jade wondered, as she lay rudely opened for Serita's inspection. Yet no sound of protest or dissidence left her lips, and she did not move other than to wriggle her hips slightly.

"On your belly."

Jade gratefully twisted over and pressed her head against the silk sheet. It was better for her like this, for they could not see her face now. But her buttocks were already being caressed by Serita's little hands. Jade's muscles leapt as she felt a finger touch her anus. The invading digit slipped inside her, causing little shivers to course down her spine.

Then Serita pressed on the inside of each of Jade's knees, forcing them apart and high above waist level, so that she lay almost in a crouch, like a frog ready to jump. She knew that her ripe sex would be hanging open, displayed, and that her buttocks were surely spread apart to reveal the puckered orifice there.

"Push your bottom up, little slut," Serita crooned, one hand pushing under Jade's belly and the other pressing down upon the slave's shoulders.

Jade complied, as she must, repelled though she was, arching her back as if begging for ravishment. When Serita gathered the leaves of Jade's sex, squeezing them together, it seemed to the tormented woman that love juices oozed out, hot and sticky. Jade gasped. The pleasure within her was rising, rising ever more. The tingling in her sensitised nipples was becoming unbearable, and her breasts seemed to swell as if to burst.

"You see," Jade heard Serita tell the Host as if in triumph. "The little slut prefers the discipline of a strong woman."

Jade was horrified. "No," she wanted to shout, "no, no, it isn't true."

"Place her in the mask," said the Host.

Serita exhaled in exasperation. However, hoisting Jade's head up by the hair, she quickly slipped the clammy leather over her face. Jade bit upon the gag that was incorporated into the leather lining of the mask, and felt the cushioned pads being nestled against her ears. Everything was blackness now and she could only hear the rustling of the leather as the mask was buckled tightly at the back of her head.

It was a snug fit: Jade could see or hear nothing. She lay there upon her belly, her knees widely splayed and buttocks upraised, feeling the sensuous silk upon her breasts. Then, without warning, pain exploded across her bottom.

The paddle!

She wriggled in desperation. It seemed so different this time, so much more painful and stark in the darkness and silence. Was it Serita who wielded the paddle she wondered miserably. She tensed in her soundless darkness, and sure enough the vicious splat across her buttocks came twice more.

Then, when Jade least expected it, as she quivered in anticipation of the next blow, her vagina was brutally entered. She arched back even more, shamelessly eager for the hard, rampaging cock. Its rhythm slowed, and Jade rotated her bottom in time with the steady thrusts.

What were they saying about her now?

After her utter ravishment, when the mask was removed, Jade found that Serita had left the room. A valet hauled her upright from the bed where the Host lounged, naked and content.

"Now we see who you prefer," he said, almost with affection. "Away with you now. You must begin your service in the taverna tomorrow."

Upon the valet's command, Jade dropped to her knees and crawled from the room. The Taverna! What would await her there?

CHAPTER THIRTEEN

The small taverna beside the quay was not all that it seemed. Outwardly, it could have been any taverna in any Greek island resort: a tamarisk tree, white paint banding its gnarled trunk, provided the scattering of battered wooden tables with scant shade. Short, stunted grass was scorched brown by the fierce sun and bright red geraniums in pots tumbled in profusion about a low wall. But those who took their leisure there were privileged with a very particular kind of service.

"Your wine, Sir," Jade said as she leaned forward to place a bottle and glasses upon a table. A fine leash, attached to her red collar, draped over her shoulder.

"No! Not good enough," snapped the Taverna Boss. "You are offering him more than wine. Go back and do it again."

Jade, naked, collared and leashed, bit her lip but dare not protest. Trying to ignore the grinning youths who sat at the table, she collected up the bottle and glasses. Returning to the gloom of the taverna room, she turned, paused, braced herself, and then came seductively forward, out into the warm sunlight again.

"Your wine, Sir," she breathed, leaning forward to proffer her pierced and bangled nipples before the men.

"Do not pull back," the Taverna Boss yelled as one of the men reached to stroke her inner thigh. "Continue to pour the wine. Smile, damn you."

"Yes, Sir," Jade whispered, as the fingers insistently brushed against her shorn sex.

"Little slut," Serita sneered as she watched from a nearby table. "You must learn to surrender to the touch of free people, even to peasants such as these."

The Taverna Boss looked across sharply. He was unaccustomed to supervision when inducting slaves into their servitude in his tavernas.

"The locals may touch within reason," he conceded, "but they cannot use the women without permission."

"Pig!" Serita snorted. "It is I who will say how this slut is prostituted. You" - she addressed the man who stroked Jade - "take her into the taverna and do as you will with her!"

The young Greek grinned happily at his colleagues and, grasping Jade's wrist, dragged her into the taverna. Inside, Sebastian, quite naked, sat on his haunches leaning against the wall, a long gleaming chain leading from his collar. And in the corner, a girl scrubbed the floor with such vigour that her delightfully pendent breasts swayed with the effort. Angelique, the black girl, fussed about polishing tables. The man hurried Jade towards one of the curtained alcoves that were banked around the walls of the taverna room, stacked three high and accessed by ladders.

When the heavy drapes were drawn Jade saw that the compartment was barely large enough for its purpose: some two metres in length and one metre in width, with a very low ceiling that necessitated crawling; it was dimly-lit by a small lamp.

An array of confinement devices hung upon the rear wall: chains, manacles, gags...

It was Jade's first acquaintance with the claustrophobic little chambers and she writhed helplessly, ankles cuffed and secured, widely-spaced, tied to hooks in the ceiling directly above her head. The young Greek was virile but, lacking finesse and experience, he took her quickly and roughly. Then he left her, still splayed and secured in the alcove. Jade, feeling the man's seed spilling from her sex, squirmed unsated in the chains. She remained thus for some minutes, her vagina aching with need, before the curtain opened and the Taverna Boss peered between her widely spread legs.

He smiled as he climbed into the alcove, his rough stubble grazing Jade's flesh. This one was vastly-experienced, and hard with his women too. Jade was allowed no respite. She served the Taverna Boss fully and comprehensively. Took pleasure from it, even from being thrashed. Her throaty moans were loud and ecstatic. Later, he roughly hauled her from the alcove and Jade hung her head when she saw the chained Sebastian smile knowingly as she passed.

"The fellow was right," the Taverna Boss told Serita when outside. "She is not exceptional. Not yet."

"Whip her then."

"The whip - your answer to all things," he snorted derisively. "Perhaps you, too, have much to learn. There are other ways to improve a woman. Girl" - he called to Angelique - "bring me the breast cups."

The black girl shuddered at his words and her hands involuntarily flew to the dark maroon tips of her ample breasts.

He laughed, but they were not for her his time.

Angelique quickly regained her composure and hurried into the taverna. She soon returned carrying a contraption of leather straps attached to two small hemispheres of black rubber, shaped like miniature breasts.

"On all fours," the man brusquely ordered Jade, shaking out the straps to reveal the facsimile of a very small brassiere. "This achieves many purposes," he told Serita as he stood astride the kneeling woman. "It teaches discipline because it is very painful for a woman to wear. She is not eager to wear it again. Is that not correct, Angelique?"

"Yes, Master," the black girl whispered, and on closer examination Serita could see dark fading marks upon the girl's breasts.

"Also, the device extends a woman's nipples" - he paused to indicate the moulded projection at the apex of each cup - "forcing them fully outwards."

Serita saw that the swollen buds which tipped Angelique's breasts were indeed remarkably protuberant, thrusting outwards like rounded pegs.

"The effect is permanent?"

"Sure." He stooped to pass the straps under Jade's chest. "I can improve almost every woman in this way. Perhaps you would care to try them yourself?"

"Pig! Get on with your work. The rings... it will not damage the creature?"

"No, although it may hurt her more than usual."

The boss positioned the small cups beneath Jade's pendent breasts, ensuring that each half-globe fitted centrally before cinching the leather straps about her back. The cups were considerably smaller than her breasts and they were held tightly against the soft, squashed flesh. Once satisfied at the positioning, he reached under the girl to squeeze air from each of the rubber moulds. Then, with one knee pressing down between her shoulder blades, he pulled strongly upon the straps.

Jade gasped as suction drew her soft flesh into the barely-yielding rubber moulds. She could feel her nipples being drawn into the vacuum at the tip of each cup. Sweating profusely with the effort, the boss stepped away from Jade and told her to stand.

"Ah, my poor little slut," Serita crooned with some satisfaction. "That is very uncomfortable for you, yes?"

"Yes, Mistress," Jade gasped, biting her lip and looking down to survey her grotesquely distorted breasts overflowing from the cups.

The Taverna Boss laughed again. "It is nothing yet. The pain builds with time and soon she will be begging for release. Then, when she begs, I tighten it further. There is an added bonus: a woman's sensitivity and desires are dramatically enhanced. Don't ask me why, but it is so."

Serita smiled and she pulled Jade's head down onto her shoulder, stroking the flaxen hair. Her other hand was held low with the index finger upraised. Jade obediently raised her body and nestled her shorn love-mound into the cup of the Spanish woman's small palm. She shuddered slightly as the upraised digit slid into her still moist slit.

"She will serve in the taverna this evening," the Taverna Boss said. "Does she dance well?"

Late evening. Still warm and sultry. The taverna was busy, for guests often preferred its quaint atmosphere to that of Big Hall. Sally Clark's body moved to a wild rhythm, caught in the music, swirling in the tight confines of the bare, polished floor.

It was here that many of the organisation's girls first learned to dance for a critical audience. Utterly nude, Sally abandoned herself to the increasing tempo. The Taverna Boss - everyone called him that - nodded his satisfaction and laid down his whip. Elsewhere, naked and leashed taverna girls scurried to and fro, serving drinks and simple meals and accepting any intimate caress or pinch that might amuse the customers she served or passed close by.

Sebastian served there too. He was a great hit with the guests, men and women. Sometimes the Taverna Boss would have Sebastian plugged with a huge phallus, embedded deep in his anus, and then his cock would rise to magnificent proportions. Like Sally, Sebastian seemed to glory in the abuse - a natural slave, perhaps. What sort of people are we? Sally often wondered. Perhaps it is a dark, secret part of everyone's sexuality?

Many of the alcoves were concealed by curtains and in use; frequently Sebastian or a waitress would put aside the serving trays and precede a guest to one of these small recesses. Sally knew that, if her performance was satisfactory, she would be immediately required to perform a more intimate dance beneath a demanding guest. If not, then there would be a whipping. She strove for perfection.

Jade was a particular attraction that night - her first evening in the taverna. Not only was she a freshly-available acquisition, and a notorious one at that, but the ring at her clitoris was an exotic extra. She wore rings in her nipples, too, but they were hidden by the punishment device she wore about her breasts.

The suffering of a woman wearing the cups seemed to excite dulled appetites. Poor Jade! Sally knew what it was like to wear those rubber cups for days on end, with breasts throbbing and bruised and, all the time, with a curious, demanding warmth in her belly. And afterwards there was the pain of release, when blood flowed back into the crushed breasts... it was exquisite. Sally's nipples were still long and thick, like thumb tips, weeks after the punishment.

She shuddered for Jade, knowing that the woman's stint of slavery at the taverna would not be easy. And, for most slaves during their time at the taverna, there were the meter boxes that had to be worked. But Jade was a special acquisition, so perhaps they would spare her that. The pampered rich bitch, Sally often thought bitterly. None of the common acquisitions, men or women, liked these specials. Why should they be any different from the rest? As it transpired, though, Jade was not spared the humiliation of working on a meter.

"No, you pig!" Serita protested. "Jade is a special acquisition."

"Specials are treated no differently," said the Head Valet. "We sell them all in one way or another."

A slim metal box now hung from Jade's collar. Then, a long chain leash was also attached to it.

"Remove your tunic," the Head Valet ordered.

Unquestioningly, Jade slipped the garment from her body and she stood before them, stark naked. Then the Head Valet gave her an ensemble that consisted of ragged strips of cloth. It was a parody of a garment; no matter how she moved, it fell aside to display more than it concealed. He manacled her hands behind her back.

"Sally," he called.

Sally Clark, clothed, hurriedly responded to the call, anxious not to lose the status that she temporarily enjoyed. Her stint of dancing in the taverna and plying for trade in the complex - whoring, no less - had been so successful that they had rewarded her with a sort of supervisory status. Sally still had to serve, of course, and abjectly, but it was better than hawking herself around the grounds.

She saw Jade waiting with the Head Valet and Serita, looking positively stunning, clad in a ragged working costume. Jade's full breasts, recently reshaped, peeked through the strips, and belled rings pierced her nipples. Sally felt immeasurably superior, for they had allowed her a short loose skirt and a buttoned blouse. She somehow felt incredibly wholesome against the wantonly-dressed Jade.

"I will report you to the Host," Serita told the Head Valet.

"This is a business," he replied. Then he turned to Sally. "Take her on the rounds. Her time is metered at treble the usual. Understand?"

Sally gulped. Treble charge? He referred to the price computed on the small meter that hung around Jade's neck. When working the complex, all meter girls wore such a device. Each guest had a personal plastic charge card and services were added to the bills of those who used the slave.

"Do I have whip rights over her?" Sally asked.

The Head Valet laughed, handing her a small dog whip. "If she fails to earn her triple quota, then she is to be whipped," he said. "Yes, beat her if need be."

Jade looked up sharply, angrily, but she made no comment as Sally led her from the building and out into bright sunlight. The bright box about the slave's neck attracted immediate attention, even before the pair had left the main complex. A guest stepped into their path and Sally immediately ordered Jade to kneel.

"Isn't this the woman who absconded?" the man asked, drawing aside the ragged strips of Jade's costume and revealing her shaven sex. "They are using her as a meter girl?"

"Her time is triple, Master."

"Robbers!" the man laughed, taking the leash. He produced a plastic card and inserted it into the slot at the top of the box affixed to Jade's collar. Then Jade found herself roughly pulled into the shrubbery. Sally sat on the grass to wait. However, within minutes, a dishevelled and perspiring Jade emerged from the shrubs. Sally could not believe it.

"Too long!" she screeched.

"What do you mean?"

"Stupid... don't you realise that the punters are being charged for your time? You have six hours to fill at triple time. At this rate, you would need eighteen customers!"

Jade gulped in amazement. "Eighteen?"

Perhaps it was because Sally feared the lash if she failed, but immediately she began to belabour Jade's thighs and calves with her whip. The beaten slave squealed and hopped about frantically, trying to avoid the stinging lashes.

"You'll do it the same as the rest of us, rich bitch," Sally snarled. "Think of yourself as a taxi. There is a standard charge for the ride and your meter clocks up according to the minutes."

"My God!" Jade breathed, rubbing her reddened thighs.

"Don't worry," he said grimly, ripping aside the fastening on Jade's costume to leave just a few ribbons of cloth draped either side of her perfect breasts. "Six hours on your meter is going to be hard work, but we can do it."

"We?" Jade asked petulantly, the bells on her nipples shaking with her anger.

"It's my job to make sure that you do not slack."

"How dare you? You are what they call a common girl, aren't you?"

Sally's satisfying reply was a sharp lash across Jade's breasts, and a knotted thong stings terribly there. Although Jade rubbed the fiery mark and glowered with hate, her nipples, sensitised by the piercing, perceptibly hardened. At that moment, two more guests approached, chatting idly as they walked in the morning sun.

"May I speak?" Sally called. When the men stopped, she dragged Jade towards them and meaningfully hefted one of the woman's bared breasts. "Buy the time of a special acquisition, Sirs. As you can see, she is specially prepared. It is triple time but she is worth it."

The men eyed Jade critically and then both shook their heads. Perhaps they had only recently emerged from their beds after a night of exhausting pleasure. The guests walked on and Sally rewarded Jade with another sharp crack of the whip.

"Stupid lazy cow! You're supposed to be looking for business, not just standing there like a sack of potatoes."

"Oh God!" Jade wept, twisting to evade the lash.

The day did not go well. Jade was unskilled at approaching guests and few were willing to pay triple price for her services. After some four hours of parading the various tourist spots on the island, only six units had been clocked on the meter. Sally was worried: if Jade's meter was returned to the Head Valet with less than eighteen units clocked then she, Sally, would be severely dealt with. Time was ticking by. Something had to be done. Anxious to avoid undue punishment, the erstwhile mistress quickly made a decision.

"We'll have to go for quantity. It will not be a pleasant day for a poor little rich girl, but what does it matter so long as we get you fucked twelve more times in the next two hours?"

"Twelve?" Jade wailed.

"Run!"

"What?"

"Run. High-step along in front of me, just as in the Dungeon. We must go for a different kind of presentation. Run!"

Sally's whip curled about Jade's thighs and, reluctantly, the near-naked girl began to prance along. Her breasts bounced and the little bell between her legs tinkled merrily as Sally unmercifully drove her in a wide circuit of the waterfront square. This was always a popular place midway through the afternoon and it was thronged with visitors. Guests and other women looked on with amusement. Presently, Sally ordered Jade to a halt.

"Buy the time of this beautiful special," Sally began her sales pitch. "Standard meter time for ten minutes with a special!"

A few guests approached, casually inspecting the heavily breathing young woman who stood there with her head bowed, weeping softly. Sally continued her harangue and presently managed to gather a small crowd. Then she ordered Jade: "Jump on the spot."

"Oh, no!"

"Lazy, pampered slut," Sally scolded, whipping Jade about the breasts and stomach, all the time calculating the effect upon potential customers. "Jump!"

Weeping, Jade did as she was bid, jumping halfheartedly on the balls of her feet. When Sally's whip bit again, she leapt higher. The bell tinkled between her legs. Sally, too, had once had to jump in this manner, and she well knew the sense of utter humiliation that Jade was experiencing. Sally also knew how guests responded to such a sight.

"Which of you Masters will exercise her for me?"

"Standard charge? You were asking triple."

"That's only if you exceed ten minutes, Sir."

"Triple?" A murmur of shock went through the crowd.

"You can surely be quick, Master?"

Immediately there were two takers. Jade was almost pathetically grateful. Breathing heavily, she smiled as the first fellow inserted his card into her meter before pulling her into the taverna. Sally followed. Ignoring the nude taverna girl, the guest swiftly bent Jade forward over a table and took her in a rough and brutal fashion. The man was done well within his allotted ten minutes. He ordered Jade to remain in position, bent forward over the table. When the man had gone, the taverna girl looked down at Jade and thoughtfully wiped the inside of her thighs with a damp cloth.

The next fellow was less demanding. He ordered Jade to kneel to pleasure him with her lips; she quickly aroused his slumbering member and brought him to an early orgasm. It was perhaps too quick for the man, because he roughly cuffed her ear after metering his card.

By once more running Jade around the square, Sally was able to sell her to two more men in the next hour. The guests knew that a special acquisition was invariably the abducted spouse of a very wealthy and powerful man, and her slavery was therefore all the more exciting to them. Jade performed abjectly for the two customers, one of whom used a painful tie to hold her helplessly splayed. Sally watched all of this, anxious that they did not exceed their ten minutes. But they were still short of units on the meter and time was running out.

"Triple is too much," a man said when Sally tried to revert to her original mission, desperately anxious to achieve the target.

Suddenly, without really thinking, Sally offered:

"Anyone who wants to have a long and leisurely experience of a lifetime can have me, too," she declared. "The meter girl is charged at triple time and I come free. Isn't that a good deal?"

It was a good offer. Sally knew that herself to be good value beneath a man.

"Two of us could share the pair of you?" one fellow asked.

"We haven't seen you," another pointed out. "Strip yourself if you are on offer, girl."

Sally hesitated. Her hard-won authority as meter mistress was proclaimed by the fact that she was clothed.

"I can't go nude while my meter girl has clothing, even if she only has a few strips of rag."

"Pity," the man said, shrugging and turning to move away.

"No, wait," Sally called, quickly unbuttoning the blouse and removing it to reveal her breasts. "I will just retain the skirt."

"Let me see what you have beneath it."

Reluctantly Sally raised the loose skirt above her waist. "Which two gentlemen will take this special rich bitch and me?" she asked, turning to display her apple-like buttocks.

Two fellows glanced inquiringly at each other and shook their heads. A man and woman stood to the side and Sally saw their eyes linger upon her breasts. The woman guest was tall and statuesque with short-cropped bottle-blonde hair.

"Okay," the woman said. "Both of you, hurry into the taverna."

Sally looked up in surprise. Her authority as meter mistress meant nothing now. She darted towards the taverna door, dragging Jade with her, not wishing to invite a beating for tardiness. The woman and her partner strode after the slaves. Inside, in the dim light, Jade and Sally waited with fearful apprehension.

"Give me the whip," the woman said, taking it from Sally and shaking out the lash. "You!" the woman ordered Jade. "Take off her skirt."

"Certainly mistress," Jade said and she smiled as she reached to remove Sally's last garment.

The woman guest then approached, licking her lips, a plastic payment card poised. Jade flinched involuntarily as the mistress reached forward to hold the meter box and insert her card into the slot. Meanwhile, the man, her partner, spoke with the Taverna Boss, who leaned on his bar watching the proceedings with interest. The Boss nodded and sauntered away. Almost immediately music wafted into the room - slow, sensuous music.

"Hold each other closely," the woman commanded.

Sally hesitatingly took Jade into her arms and she felt a little shudder as their naked flesh came into contact. Their breasts seemed almost to stick together as they pressed against each other and Sally could feel Jade's nipple rings against her own soft flesh. How would it feel to be so adorned? Sally wondered. Then a sharp pain fired across Jade's buttocks and her body jerked in Sally's arms. They found each other tightly hugging.

"Caress each other. Lower. Now, kiss... a long, lingering kiss."

Sally dared a glance over her shoulder but she could not refuse. Closing her eyes, she diffidently touched Jade's full, bee-stung lips. Jade responded, and the two kissed deeply. It was a delicious new sensation to Sally and she sensed Jade responding too. The nude slave's caresses became more urgent and Sally suddenly encountered Jade's probing tongue. The rich bitch was more sensual than Sally had credited.

"Charming," the man said.

"Delightful," his partner agreed, hitching up her skirt to reveal a black triangle of luxuriant curls. "Each of you, put a finger into the other's arsehole. Hold each other like that." She began to caress her own, wet slit.

The air was redolent with the musky smell of feminine arousal, and the man also began slowly to masturbate. Jade let out a little moan as a forefinger penetrated her anus, and she stretched down to press her thumb against Sally's tightly puckered rose.

"Sixty-nine, don't you think, dear?" the man asked casually.

"Yes. On the floor," came the order, and Sally's heart beat wildly as she understood the implication.

The entwined slaves lowered themselves to the boards. Jade immediately twisted around to bury her head between Sally's legs, and the delicious sensation of her small darting tongue made the writhing woman melt.

Sally avidly returned the pleasure. Licking at Jade's smooth, silky nether lips, so unusual, parted like an orchid to reveal both inner and outer sets, she lightly nipped the large pierced bud between her teeth. Jade's body jerked and she thrust her hips forward to demand the invading tongue.

When the two slaves eventually returned to the Head Valet, Jade's meter box showed twenty units. He did not seem surprised either at Sally's nudity or at the high earnings.

"Go to the showers, both of you," he said, taking the meter.

They lathered each other's body under the warm stream. Despite, or perhaps because of, Sally's harsh discipline over her that day, Jade was incredibly warm and gentle. She clearly took pleasure in the arms of a woman. They kissed again and giggled.

As they were returning to their quarters, showered but weary, they passed by the Conservatory. Lights were shining from its windows and they could see male and female slaves performing there. The women, with their curious dresses of crackling taffeta that left their breasts bare, seemed particularly exotic.

"I love wearing those dresses," Jade said. "Is that shocking?"

"No."

"This whole condition is - it's exciting."

"Yes," Sally said with a slight smile. "I can see that it worries you, feeling like this."

"Oh!"

Jade stopped in surprise beside a large tree. It was lit by strategically placed floodlights and, in the bright illumination, two slaves hung from the lower branches like large bundles. They swung and twisted gently in the breeze. The ties that held them were particularly cruel: although they hung by their ankles, spread apart and held by laced cuffs, their bodies had been doubled and secured.

"Punishment," Sally shrugged, looking up at them. "They will have learned a hard lesson by morning. I'm going to bed."

Jade was fascinated. After Sally had left her there, she walked over to the tree, casting an anxious eye for valets. The slaves hung five feet from the ground, moaning occasionally in their trussed misery. Their faces peered at Jade from between their splayed legs.

"Angelique," she said, recognising the black girl. "And Sebastian!"

She saw that the sex of each was neatly displayed virtually in front of her eyes. Sebastian's cock was hard and a small globule of moisture gleamed at its tip. Angelique's beauty lips were exposed like ripe plums and they seemed to open and shut in little spasms.

112

"The meter girl," Sebastian said, irony in his voice. "Have you earned your keep?"

"Shut up," Angelique scolded, spinning slowly on the bough. "Aren't we in trouble enough?"

Jade found herself reaching for Sebastian's cock and stroking it gently. "What have you done to deserve this?" she asked, half to herself.

Sebastian groaned as Jade gently worked the foreskin back from the large, purple head of his penis. She smiled up into his face, almost maliciously. Relations between the two had deteriorated badly in the past weeks. "Well?" she asked, her fingernail on the tender exposed skin.

"We were caught fucking together," Sebastian said bitterly.

"Angelique?"

"Yes, that's all it was."

Jade heard herself chuckle throatily. The absurdity of it all made her laugh. Why, she herself had been fucked so often that day, working the meter. And Sebastian had been put to her on more than one occasion. Slaves were frequently required to rut together for the pleasure of voyeuristic guests and in training.

"Bad slave," she said with a mocking smile, turning Sebastian with his penis before walking away. "I thought that you were the one who loved to obey your masters."

CHAPTER FOURTEEN

The Host had his masters like everyone else. They were shadowy figures, these people who had financed his organisation and who now took care to protect their lucrative investment.

"What have you done about this American mobster who is wrecking our clubs?" the man who had come demanded angrily.

The Host eyed him coolly, even with a touch of arrogance. "The matter is in hand. I intend to obtain handsome recompense from Mr Felix Tranter.

"First the Bond-Age in London and now the Whipround in Amsterdam. He has to be stopped. I will make the necessary arrangements -"

"No!" the Host said sharply.

The man sighed in exasperation. He looked questioningly across the desk, squinting in the sunlight that streamed through the window. The Host had hitherto been a reliable and clever servant. There had been signs that he was beginning to make mistakes but perhaps that could happen to anyone. Other associates had begun to ask questions and were demanding changes. They argued that the organisation's business could be expanded to include other activities which interested the backers. The Host had always resisted demands that he use his organisation to deal in drugs, the Mafia's modern business commodity. He was old-fashioned in many ways, and steadfastly continued to ply the family's traditional and long-established trade in white slaves.

"Time is running out," the man said. "My friends are restless."

When the man had left, the Host reflected on his words. How dare these men threaten him in such a way? He reached into the top drawer of his desk and took out the long, razor-sharp knife he habitually kept there. For some minutes he was lost in thoughts of deep overriding anger. Fingering the shining blade, he made imaginary slashing motions across his wrist; he then held the point to his belly, pricking the slight paunch through his silk shirt. Long moments later he cackled with manic laughter. Others must pay, not he! Taking up a nearby telephone he rasped an order:

"Lily! Fetch Lily!"

Within minutes a fearful Lily stood before his desk, eyes downcast, bared breasts swiftly rising and falling above the yellow faille of her gown. The long belled skirt of crackling, stiff taffeta was hitched up at the front, rolled and falling into heavy diagonal folds to reveal a thin blue-black line traced at the top of her exposed thighs. The Host approached her, knife in hand. He further parted the curtaining of her skirt and teased her silken, pubic thatch with the tip of the blade. Lily stood stock still, hardly daring to breath as he scratched her soft stomach with the cold, deadly metal; she imagined the sensation of trickling blood but could not be sure.

"They are trying to depose me!" the Host said at last. "You are an accomplice."

"No! Oh no!"

"No? Perhaps not. I intend to get my revenge against those who seek to harm me. This is my organisation, my island. I created it, like a Greek god. Should I kill you, Lily?"

"I think you are tired," she stammered. "You are the Host and I have always been loyal to you."

He gazed at her naked thighs for long minutes, idly toying with the knife against her skin. Presently, he spoke again. "Yes! I am the Host! And the Host is a man of honour. I pay my debts. You shall be recompensed. You must take over the Whipround in Amsterdam - there is much to be done there. Go! You must leave the island today. My loyal subjects are no longer safe here."

Gratefully, the woman hurried from the Host's office, her skirts crackling as she fled. He was becoming mad! Just as readily, perhaps, he would have plunged the knife into her belly. Lily hurried to her quarters and changed the silken gown for a smart business suit. Then she waited anxiously for transport from the island, fearing that the madman would change his mind.

At that moment the Host was giving instructions to his secretary. "Invite Felix Tranter and John Preston to the island," he ordered. "Arrange it."

Tranter's invitation arrived by special delivery. It was tastefully printed on hand-crafted paper but, curiously, gave little information. Some days later, a woman contacted Felix and enticed him with a vivid description of the delights offered by the exclusive resort. He would be collected and transported, with all expenses paid. It was a very special invitation, she explained.

When John Preston received a similar contact at his villa in Istanbul he immediately telephoned the Policeman, who hastily flew to Turkey to meet with him.

"I want you to find this woman," the Policeman said, producing a small photograph from a leather wallet.

It was a picture of a girl: blonde, attractive, laughing.

"Am I supposed to know her?"

"That young woman is a prisoner on the island," the Policeman said. "I want you to get her out and take her to London. Buy her if there is no other way - I have the necessary funds. It is very important."

The two men then retired to the courtyard, where they could make their plans.

"You must be prepared for a shock when you meet your wife," the Policeman warned Preston. "My informant, has recently returned from the island, and she tells me that Jade has changed both physically and mentally. It seems that the Host has taken a particular fancy for her."

"Oh!" Jade yelped, her buttocks seared by Serita's cane.

"You may be The Host's favourite slut," Serita said, "but in the training room that means nothing. Keep up with the others."

"Yes, Mistress."

Carlos Fernandez peered through the one-way mirror with both fascination and satisfaction. Serita, his wife, was relentlessly and mercilessly putting a number of young men and women through their paces in the training room. The nude slaves perspired freely as they strove to satisfy her demands and thus avoid the stinging cane which she used freely and frequently.

"Move, sluts," Serita called, as the tempo of the music changed. "Follow Natasha. Keep up with her now." Her cane again caught Jade across the thighs as she struggled to maintain the pace set by the Russian athlete. "Jade, let me hear that bell - not so tardy now."

Natasha, naked like the others, faced the group and led them in a demanding routine. Carlos critically eyed her trim buttocks and firm, athletic body. She had returned to full fitness and positively glowed with health. The once fiery Natasha was now pliant to Serita's every command.

"Stop. Rest. Natasha make you work, uh? Jade, come, my pretty one."

Serita, her arm straight down her side, held out her hand, palm uppermost. Jade inhaled deeply; the Spanish woman loved to humiliate her in this way to demonstrate her mastery. However, always, the demand aroused a deep, fluttering feeling within Jade's belly. She moved forward and, rising onto her toes, positioned her smooth sex onto the waiting hand; only a slight tremor betrayed any emotion as the clawed digits cruelly penetrated her.

"I have you all in my hand, uh?" Serita gloated, applying pressure and forcing the young woman to turn, still impaled. Then, withdrawing her hand, she thrust her fingers into Jade's mouth.

"Excellent," Carlos Fernandez chuckled.

"Indeed!" said the Host, standing beside him in the viewing room. "Serita has a natural talent. I will be almost sad to lose her from my training staff."

"Ah, but we have an arrangement. She has also been allowed to indulge her desires with men?"

"Oh, most certainly. There are some painful scores to settle. I can well understand your wish to reconfigure her character."

The handsome Carlos smiled darkly as he continued to watch his wife through the glass. She was now cruelly belabouring a woman with her cane. "She very nearly castrated me, you know," he said. "I would divorce the bitch but her family could damage me permanently. It is better this way."

"It will be done," replied the Host.

"When?"

"Tonight, in Big Hall."

That night in Big Hall seemed much like any other: a heady mix of erotic pleasure.

"Wine, Sir?" a woman breathed, leaning forward to proffer the flagon. The sheer gauze fabric she wore concealed nothing of her beauty, but merely enhanced her nudity. All of the wine carriers were clad in the same manner. The guest scarcely looked up as he held out a glass. Pouting a little, aware of the eyes of the Head Valet upon her, the woman poured the wine before replacing the flagon upon her right shoulder and walking elegantly to the next table.

Natasha had been given a different task. Along with a team of other slaves, she greeted guests as they arrived and escorted them into Big Hall. She wore a parody of a conventional long evening gown: black velvet, clinging to every curve, but topless and with a skirt slit widely to the belly, way above her shorn sex lips. Black gloves almost to her armpits, sheer black stockings and very high heeled shoes completed the breathtaking picture. Natasha's pale flesh and blonde hair contrasted starkly with the black clothing. Her breasts moved liquidly, and long lissome legs flashed as she led each group of guests across the large room.

Angelique knelt at the feet of a large bearded fellow who idly fondled her magnificent black breasts while in conversation with other guests. Gunther, the handsome blond German, was locked in the embrace of a middle-aged woman who unabashedly fondled his large, erect organ. Another female slave, stark naked, lay stretched upon a chaise longue as a man carefully poured wine into her navel before lapping it up, repeating the process time and again.

In an alcove a wine girl was bent over a table, gasping, her gauze drape rucked high as a man took his pleasure with mighty thrusts of his huge weapon. Jade looked on with a shudder, realising that it might have been her clutching the table and grinding her hips onto the massive cock. She she would surely be raped during the evening, probably more than once. And in what humiliating circumstances? Eventually, when the man had discharged his lust, the girl straightened, smiled shyly, and adjusted the filmy material about her body. Flushed and perspiring, she hoisted the wine flagon onto her shoulder and hurried towards the exit.

The serving girls were frequently used by many guests each night. They were often ordered into the gardens and taken roughly, writhing on the grass under the stars. This applied to the male slaves too, of course, for the organisation catered for all tastes.

"Move," a valet ordered Jade, tapping her with his cane.

A tawny beauty clad in a demure white gown entered Big Hall: Serita, wife of the multimillionaire Spanish financier and, it was rumoured, a minor member of the Bourbon royal family. Two nude men - Sebastian and another - escorted her. She was here not as a mere trainer, it seemed, but an honoured guest!

Natasha, her free breasts bouncing prettily, led the group to a table. Serita walked proudly and defiantly, a haughty smile on her face. She strode purposefully between the deferential male slaves. Serita did not affect the elegant glide or downcast fluttering eyelashes of the collared women. All acquisitions, male and female, had suffered cruelly at the hands of the Spanish aristocrat; she revelled in their degradation.

"Mistress," Natasha said, pulling out a chair.

"Slut!" Serita sniffed as the Russian's gown separated to reveal the deep cleft at the top of her thighs.

"Bitch!" Natasha exclaimed, then put a horrified hand to her mouth.

"Natasha!" barked a nearby trainer. "Apologise and then report to the Head Valet."

"I am so sorry, Mistress."

"My compliments to the Head Valet," Serita said with a wave of dismissal. "After your punishment, I wish to see the stripes."

Natasha fled, fighting back tears. Jade yelped suddenly as a valet's cane rapped sharply upwards to the rise of her buttocks. She had been tardy, forgetting her duties. Hurrying forward, the wine flagon on her shoulder, Jade approached Serita. "Wine, mistress?"

"Well, well!" Serita said. "Another pretty little thing ready to serve her masters."

"Yes, Mistress."

"You should try this one," Serita told her companions. "She is hot."

"Will that be all, Mistress?" Jade whispered after she had poured the wine.

"She is good, you say?"

"Superb."

"Put down the flagon and remove that rag."

Inhaling deeply, Jade did as she was bid, and stood provocatively naked, eyes down-cast, hands behind her back. Her pierced and ringed nipples invariably caught the eye, as did the small glistening ring that protruded from the leaves of her sex.

"One of our specials, as you can see from her red collar and lack of body hair. They are as available as the rest of the sluts."

"Come here, girl," the man said. "Kneel beside me."

When Natasha returned she saw Jade, stark naked, kneeling beside one of the men, her head on his lap as he stroked her hair. The Russian was also naked to all intents and purposes: her gown had been removed, leaving nothing but long black gloves, stockings and high stiletto-heeled shoes. Her eyes were reddened by tears.

"Mistress," she said quietly, dutifully turning and bending to display the rosy, fiery hue of a well-beaten bottom.

"It is not enough," Serita said, warming her hand on the glowing flesh. "Once more, harder, then report to the Dungeon."

Tearfully, Natasha began to walk away. At that moment Sebastian hurried to Serita and whispered into her ear. She frowned petulantly but nodded.

"I am afraid that this one is spoken for tonight," she told the man who was toying with Jade's breasts.

"How is that so?"

"Instructions of the Host," Serita said. Then she called: "Natasha!"

The Russian woman stopped and, seeing Serita's beckoning finger, she returned to stand before the hated woman.

"As you can see, Natasha is also a special acquisition. The wife of a notorious gangster, I believe. Take her instead. You won't be disappointed. Isn't that so, Natasha?"

"Yes, Mistress."

The man reluctantly pushed Jade away. He sighed and beckoned Natasha to his couch. She sank gratefully into his arms, nuzzling her head against his shoulder. It was certainly preferable to another beating and a night in the rat-cellar.

Jade collected her flagon and hurried away. She knew she would serve the Host again that night. Again! He was using her with increasing frequency. Jade could not understand it but the awesome leader was obviously smitten with her.

It did not excuse her from the duties in Big Hall. She remained naked from then on that night, her exotic hardware on show. It was quite usual. Indeed, in Big Hall, Jade's statuesque body was only rarely clad, even in the revealing clothing of a serving girl. Bells tinkled on her nipples and clitoris as she swayed from table to table.

The Host graciously accepted wine from her flagon. As she stooped to pour, he caressed her and whispered into her ear. She smiled and nodded before hurrying to the next table.

Serita glowered when next she saw Jade. She grasped one of the nipple rings and twisted it painfully. "You visit the Host again tonight, little slut?"

"Yes, Mistress."

"He likes his ugly duckling who is now a swan, uh? Is it the rings and bells? I think, perhaps, it is so."

Jade winced as the woman sharply tugged on the nipple ring. She knew that Serita would be particularly harsh the next day. The Spanish woman would find some excuse to beat her soundly: it was always so when the Host called upon Jade to share his bed. Share his bed? Frequently, Jade slept curled on the floor, chained, deprived of hearing and sight in the clammy mask. She was becoming accustomed to it, even secretly delighting in anticipation of the exquisite ordeal. Still Serita held her by the nipple ring, and she stooped, her breast throbbing.

"The Head Valet wishes to see you in Reception, Mistress," Sebastian came to tell Serita, glancing with a smile at Jade's distended breast.

The Spanish beauty sighed. She excused herself from the guests and, as she left, spotlights followed Sally Clark as she walked to the centre of the room, feet clattering loudly upon the birchwood floor with each step; wrists manacled behind her, she was naked except for beribboned shoes with metal tips on toes and heels. The Head Valet usually introduced this diversion but, on this occasion, one of his subordinates attended the girl, cane at the ready. Guests, familiar with the entertainment, cheered.

Six young men followed Sally to the centre of the room. Not slaves these, but locals... their muscular darkly tanned bodies clad only in loin cloths. Guests watched avidly as the girl eyed them. Sally's belly fluttered with a perverse excitement as guests struck wagers amidst avid argument and light banter. She had never before been run in Big Hall but she had seen other girls do it.

Her eyelashes fluttered provocatively at each of the men in turn. Which of them would win her? The men separated and moved to various points on the large dance floor. They were then blindfolded.

"Oh!"

Although expecting it, the sharp cut of the cane still surprised Sally and she fled away from the valet, a loud clip of metal upon wood accompanying her every step. She knew that the blindfolded men would be listening intently, trying to gauge her position. Sally stopped stock still, as she knew she must, when the valet blew a whistle and the men began their search.

Under pain of the cane, the naked girl remained immobile as a man approached, groping blindly. He passed within a yard of her, his flailing arms almost touching her body. The whistle blew again, and Sally dutifully tripped noisily to another position. Guests were now cheering encouragement, willing favoured performers to succeed in catching her, anxious to collect on their bets.

Perhaps Sally was not good at this game. After only five moves, she was caught amidst wild cheers and simultaneous groans. The noise reached a crescendo as the man tore off his blindfold and pushed the captured woman to the floor. Sally knew what must follow and she lay back, spreading her legs to accept the man. Pulling aside his loin cloth, he leapt upon her and rapaciously claimed his prize. Money changed hands among the guests as Sally writhed beneath the man's onslaught.

Later, few seemed to notice her as she made her way from Big Hall, still naked apart from the metal-tipped shoes.

"Ladies and gentlemen," a valet announced. "We now have a special entertainment for you. We present the lovely Serita!"

Everyone gasped as Serita sped into the room. She wore a red leather body-harness, tightly buckled over her shoulders, under her breasts, round her waist and thighs. Otherwise, the beautiful and previously haughty Spanish woman was totally naked!

Each of Serita's small wrists were buckled to the straps which tightly encircled her thighs. A long leash, attached to her collar, was held by the Head Valet. He obviously relished his role, expertly wielding a long, plaited leather whip, painfully curling its tip against the fleeing woman's tender flesh.

"Previously a feared trainer," announced the valet, "but now degraded by order of her sponsor. We invite the acquisitions to form two lines on the floor."

Glancing uneasily at each other, collared men and women hurried to comply. Jade placed her wine flagon to one side and ran to stand alongside Natasha and Angelique. Sebastian, Gunther and other men were there too. In short order some forty slaves stood facing each other in two files, perhaps four feet apart. A valet wandered along the lines, issuing each of them with a light multi-thonged whip. These scourges could not inflict real damage but their thin, knotted thongs would certainly sting like scorpions. Serita, standing at the head of the lines, watched in agonised anticipation. The intention was clear and these slaves hated her!

"Run!" the Head Valet commanded, cracking his whip.

Serita hesitated but was galvanised into action when the long whip curled painfully under her legs. She darted between the lines of slaves, yelping, trying desperately to avoid their wildly swinging lashes. Within seconds, she had reached the other end of the room and the leash abruptly stopped her flight. She had escaped almost unscathed, although one or two blows had landed to stripe her body. The slaves waited eagerly, raising their whips.

"Back!"

Again Serita ran the gauntlet of flailing, viciously stinging straps. She was slower this time, secured in the harness and unable to use her hands to ward off the blows. The beaten woman squealed as viciously stinging lashes bit into her flesh. Jade took grim satisfaction in catching her tormentor with a particularly spiteful blow that made her squeal.

Sobbing for breath, the naked women slumped to the floor at the feet of the Head Valet. He quickly unsnapped the buckles which secured her wrists.

"Hands and knees," he ordered.

Her lips silently pleading, Serita nevertheless knelt on all fours, her breasts

121

hanging beautifully.

"Go!"

The Spanish beauty crawled painfully forward. Each slave had ample time to prepare and deliver three or four stinging blows. Both Jade and Natasha each managed to lay three stripes across the olive skin of Serita's exposed back and bottom. Carlos Fernandez, watching from a corner of the room, chuckled with delight. Twice his wife collapsed on her belly but the continuing hail of lashes forced her to resume her progress to the end of the lines, where she lay crumpled and sobbing.

"Enough!"

"The lady is obviously quite unpopular," the valet announced to a ripple of laughter. "We now proceed to the collaring of our latest acquisition."

Another terse order, and Serita painfully climbed to her feet. Stumbling slightly, walked to the centre of the floor. There she knelt, with widely spaced knees and her back straight. The Head Valet approached, theatrically bearing a broad leather collar and matching cuffs. Serita meekly extended her arms and the Head Valet clipped leather bracelets about her wrists. Sobbing, the beauty straightened once more and held her chin high to facilitate the fitting of a collar.

"A charming spectacle," Carlos said, stepping forward.

"You!"

"Certainly, my dear. You may no longer look into my face. You now wear a collar. That has always been your true status here. Everything else was just a delicious preliminary. I arranged it."

"So I must learn to be submissive for you. Yes?"

"What, no threats to kill me? No screaming fit of rage? No dire promises of revenge at the hands of your family?"

Serita hung her head and did not reply.

Sebastian was then led forward. There were cheers of anticipation, for he had gained something of a reputation as a capable stud. Standing before the newly-collared Serita, his cock impressively rampant, he waited quietly. The Head Trainer stooped to whisper into Serita's ear.

She shook her head wildly.

Once more the whip cracked across her shoulders, and Carlos laughed again. With a groan, Serita's tiny hands reached to take Sebastian's massive organ. Then, tossing her head slightly to remove the flowing hair from her face, she took the penis into her mouth. Again the guests cheered wildly. There was a look of triumph on Sebastian's face as Serita fellated him; like the other slaves, he had suffered often at her hands.

Later, Serita curled naked and weeping in the deep blackness of the Dungeon.

At the same time, in the Host's quarters, Jade's hearing and sight were eclipsed by the feathered mask and she waited for his touch or, perhaps, his whip; she never knew which would come first.

Meanwhile, Natasha yielded fully and energetically in the luxury of a guest's apartment although, despite the relative comfort of her surroundings, the guest allowed her neither reserve nor inhibition. Still, Natasha Tranter's accommodation was preferable to the dank Dungeon.

CHAPTER FIFTEEN

Felix Tranter surveyed his accommodation. He could not complain despite the secrecy which had made him thoroughly nervous throughout the journey. Since Athens, he had no idea where he was being taken. The helicopter transport afforded little notion of either direction or location. It was extremely discomfiting to men like Tranter and John Preston, for they were only too aware that dangerous enemies existed.

However, the presence of four other passengers was reassuring. These men were clearly wealthy and, it seemed, rather nonchalant about the whole affair. Two of them chatted amiably together: obviously old acquaintances. Preston half-expected to find the Policeman amongst the other passengers but he was not there.

"What the hell do you make of all this?" Tranter asked John Preston.

"It was an invitation I couldn't refuse."

When the helicopter finally landed the guests found themselves alighting onto a lush green lawn, welcomed by incredibly beautiful young hostesses who led each of them to a superb air-conditioned apartment. There, the pliant women made themselves fully available to the newly-arrived guests.

Preston dismissed the girl assigned to him. After freshening up, he wandered the grounds, anxious to reconnoitre the place. In his pocket was a small photograph of an attractive blonde girl, but neither she nor the other woman he sought were to be seen among those in the gardens that day.

Tranter luxuriated in a tub as a young woman, naked except for a green collar, soaped his body with timid hands.

She was utterly respectful but declined to answer any of his more pertinent questions. When the beauty knelt to towel him dry, his need was painfully apparent. The girl gently stroked his erect cock with obvious reluctance. Felix Tranter was a man of action, if rather crude and brutal. He merely hoisted the girl under his arm, carried her from the bathroom and threw her onto the bed. He expected protest, but she merely smiled shyly and spread her legs. Tranter wasted little time in ravishing her and seemingly she dared not struggle - it was the best sex he had ever experienced and he had certainly had enough of it in his time. But the women he used were cold and calculating and his wife, Natasha, although always energetic in bed, was never as compliant as this girl. Afterwards, Felix lay exhausted and contented on the bed as she washed herself in the bathroom, quietly sobbing.

There was a tap on the door and Tranter hurriedly drew a sheet across his flaccid organ as a valet entered the room.

"Compliments of the Host," the strangely garbed man said politely. "He would like to see you in his private office."

"Ah, thank you." The Host was acknowledging the Head Valet as he led a naked masked young woman into his office. "Put her on my desk, please."

Felix Tranter watched in amazement as the sightless nude docilely allowed herself to be theatrically posed. She wore an elaborate sequined mask of green yellow and purple feathers, which covered her entire head. The Head Valet took some care arranging her. Finally, she sat perched with one foot on the floor and the other upon the polished surface of the desk, back arched to thrust out her firm breasts.

"A small indulgence, Mr Tranter. It relieves my boredom and the materials are readily available, as you have seen. She is effectively prevented from seeing, hearing or speaking by the mask, so our privacy is assured."

"This place is something else!" Tranter admitted, as the Head Valet left the room.

"We like to think so. There are four strands to our business. Firstly we have the common green-collared girls: they are simply obtained, trained and sold to connoisseurs the world over. There is an auction here tomorrow, which is why you have been invited at this time."

They were interrupted by a knock on the door and Gunther, the handsome male slave, entered on command. With a nod from the Host, Gunther approached the masked woman and she started with surprise when he began to expertly caress her. Relentlessly conditioned, and now deprived of all but her tactile senses, the woman began to respond immediately.

"I understand that you have been seeking to expand your own business activities?" the Host asked Tranter.

The American, avidly watching as Gunther manipulated the naked woman, looked up sharply. He frowned, wondering how this enigmatic man knew of his dealings, but did not pursue the point. Instead he asked, "What is your second line of business?"

"This island itself. We offer a sanctuary for wealthy people who wish to indulge in their rather specialist tastes."

"So I see."

"Quite. The third strand of our business may interest you. We use the same facilities and methods to select and acquire the wives of very wealthy men. We then ransom them. This delightful creature" - he indicated the writhing woman - "is one such acquisition."

"Jeez!"

Gunther turned the woman onto her belly and she lay with her breasts squashed upon the polished surface of the desk. With strong hands around her ankles he flexed her knees and spread her thighs frog-like, holding the lissome legs perpendicular. He then thrust his massive member into her helpless slit.

"Her husband is very wealthy and extremely powerful. Such special status does not excuse her from performing full service on the island for the pleasure of myself and my guests, of course. Special acquisitions serve with the common girls. This specimen is a superb performer, as you can see. Her husband will be surprised at the change in her."

There was something in the Host's tone that disconcerted Tranter. "What's your pitch?" he demanded.

"Pitch?" The Host replied coldly. "You have been defecating on my pitch for a considerable time, Mr Tranter. The fourth strand of my organisation involves a number of business establishments in various parts of the world. The Whipround Club in Amsterdam, for example. And the Bond-Age in London."

Tranter's jaw dropped. He now vividly recalled that fateful night in the seedy Soho clip-joint. The basement cellar had been dimly-lit and his meeting with the Host that night had been so brief.

"You!" he exclaimed.

"Me! You attempted to take over the Club. Then your hired assassin took a gun to me and wounded my arm - he almost killed me. After that, your henchmen smashed the place. Then, not content, you wrecked the Wipround Club in Amsterdam. You have incurred my great displeasure, Mr Tranter."

Tranter stared incredulously. "Are you crazy?"

The Host smiled, a seemingly sad and disappointed smile. He produced a thick file and tossed it upon the leather surface; the legend 'FELIX TRANTER' was inscribed upon the cover.

Tranter stared suspiciously at the wad of papers before snatching it up from the desk-top. He began to study the dossier, glancing up briefly when the masked woman's body suddenly bucked violently as she struggled to escape Gunther's thrusts. The mobster grimaced and then returned his attention to the dossier. He numbly thumbing through its pages, realising that this sinister organisation and its mysterious leader had targeted him for more than a year.

"Somebody fingered me for attempting to kill you. Nuts! And smashing up your clubs. These reports are crap, man."

"Come, Mr Tranter!"

Gunther continued to thrust his bludgeoning weapon into the writhing nude woman. Tranter watched in fascination as she moved her lovely rear to match his thrusts. Now it seemed that the masked nude was completely lost in the throes of lust. Finally, she heaved and twisted in a mighty orgasm. The virile young man roared as he reached his own climax. Then he withdrew, leaving the woman limply sprawled over the desk.

"Ah!" The Host said with evident pleasure, and he moved to stroke the panting woman. "Remove her mask, if you please."

The woman was pulled to her feet and Gunther unbuckled her feathered headgear. Natasha Tranter blinked in the light, tossing her dishevelled, sweat-soaked main of blonde hair. Then her eyes, briefly, alighted upon Felix.

"Natasha!" Tranter croaked.

The naked, used woman stood with her head bowed, eyes averted. However, the soft tremor of her breasts suggested that she was weeping.

"Yes, Mr Tranter," the Host said with a devilish chuckle. "It is your wife. She has become an accomplished whore. This weekend we shall sell her - if not to you then to someone else."

"Why?" Tranter croaked.

"Revenge. I could have had you killed, of course. Indeed, my associates demanded it. However, this revenge is so much sweeter to me. The price of your wife, to you, Sir, is one million."

Felix Tranter gazed in disbelief, first at his ravished wife and then at the Host. "One million?" he exclaimed. "One million dollars?"

"Sterling!"

The Host recovered his dossier from the American's shaking hands. Surprisingly, there was no anger, none of the violence that had been anticipated. Just shock and, most satisfyingly to the Host, utter horror.

"All of this and you have the wrong guy," Tranter croaked. "I pay you one million in sterling and then you kill us both. Right?"

The Host looked up sharply, pained. "Mr Tranter," he said sternly, "I have invested heavily in training your wife. Am I likely to kill her now?"

The American had received a rough schooling. He had learned to recognise and mitigate defeat in the tenements of the New York ghetto. It seemed there was little option: the ransom might buy both his wife and his life, it just might. There was nothing to lose.

"Okay," Felix said heavily. "I'll pay. But you're living on borrowed time, buddy."

The Host smiled and simply handed Felix a telephone. When Tranter had called his bank in New York, the valet escorted Natasha from the room. Felix watched her go, incredulity still etched into his florid features.

"Where is he taking her now?" Tranter demanded.

"Natasha will be kept secure until I receive confirmation that the funds are transferred. She will serve our guests tonight, as usual. Does that worry you?"

"You bastard!"

The Host chuckled with delight. "If you'll excuse me," he said, "I have some business in the training room."

The training room was brightly lit. Behind the one-way viewing glass,

127

John Preston watched with, apparently, only mild interest as a nude beauty ran lightly into the training room. She was accompanied by a valet who wielded a thin cane.

"You really do not remember me, Mr Preston," the Host said genially. "Do you recall a fracas at the Bond-Age Club in London?" - he paused to roll up the sleeve of his shirt, revealing a livid scar - "You probably saved my life that night and I have been repaying you ever since."

Preston gazed at the naked woman as she posed in the centre of the room before beginning an erotic, precisely choreographed routine. Her smooth, practised performance was designed to display every facet of her delightful body.

"I see that you have my wife," he said.

"You don't seem very surprised."

"Nothing surprises me any more."

The Host frowned, concerned and nonplussed by Preston's apparent lack of emotion. However, this man was an arms dealer who had treated with despots and desperadoes the world over and that takes a special kind of nerve. He watched as John Preston coolly eyed the barbaric adornments upon Jade's nipples and clitoris.

"Her breasts are fuller now, and more beautiful. We have had her nose reshaped, too."

"What do you want from me?"

"Nothing, my dear fellow. Quite the contrary. I have personally supervised the training of your wife, improved her immeasurably. Pierced and adorned - I know you find that attractive. It is my reward. I took her, trained her, invested time and money. That is what we do here. I now return Jade to you, without cost. What more could a man want? She gave us some trouble, initially, but not now, not any more."

At that point Sebastian and Gunther entered the training room. Preston's urbane features hardened somewhat as the men, naked, stood over his wife; their arousal was in evidence.

"You must allow my little joke," the Host chuckled, seeing Preston staring at Sebastian. "Jade is no longer infatuated with him. Still, if you wish, I shall have him flogged before your eyes and sold into guaranteed misery."

"No," Preston said. "That is not necessary."

The trainer tapped Jade with his cane. She immediately rolled onto her back, her knees flexed and spread. A slight sheen of moisture, unmistakable, appeared upon her shaven sex, and her face was aglow with anticipation. Kneeling, the two men began to caress and stroke her pliant flesh and she writhed beneath their deft, practised hands. Her body arched to meet and invite the touches. Legs thrashed wildly and she tried to pull Sebastian to her. There was no mercy for Jade, however, for they continued to drive her to the very brink of crisis.

"Interesting?" the Host asked. "Note how your wife's breasts and shoulders are mottled and suffused with that rich, red blush. It is the sign that she is already approaching her first orgasm. We are experts in such things."

The erotic tableau of rapine went on for some time until Jade Preston became a begging mass of demanding flesh. Still the men made no effort to satisfy her. Instead, they worked insistently and relentlessly upon her helpless squirming body, denying any release, stroking the heat to ever greater intensity.

Finally, Sebastian moved between Jade's thighs. John Preston inhaled sharply. The slave placed his hands under Jade's buttocks and hoisted her onto his throbbing, rampant member. Preston could see how his wife gasped and groaned, not with anguish but in ecstasy. The other man knelt behind the writhing woman to raise her shoulders. Her head hung back and she hungrily took his cock into her mouth. Back arched, a living, bucking bridge suspended between the two demanding cocks, Jade rode out the storm of a mighty orgasm.

Preston watched, displaying impressive composure. "This is because I saved your life?" he asked. "You are certifiably crazy!"

Later, when Preston had left and Jade and the two male slaves had been removed, two other nude women ran into the training room. Carlos Fernandez chuckled throatily in pleasure. His wife Serita made a charming picture as she reluctantly posed before the mirror. The tawny dark-haired creature turned to reveal her freshly beaten bottom. Plainly visible, inserted into her rear orifice, was a thick ebony plug.

"Excellent," Fernandez said.

"Thank you, Senor."

Docile and tamed, Serita lay upon the floor, her knees flexed and spread. Natasha immediately straddled the woman's face, and Carlos Fernandez could clearly see his wife's little tongue flicking against the Russian beauty's nether lips.

"Most excellent," the Spanish gentleman repeated.

"Is Serita your only interest during this trip?" the Host asked.

"Perhaps I will buy, if I see the right woman."

"We have some excellent common acquisitions for sale. They will be displayed in Big Hall tomorrow."

CHAPTER SIXTEEN

Common acquisitions were on display in Big Hall. A lot number was marked in grease paint upon the right breast of each. Stark naked, carefully clipped and groomed, they stood upon low platforms some four feet square and eighteen inches high which had been arranged throughout the large room.

Selected for their beauty, plucked from streets, offices, beaches and nighteries throughout the world, once on the island, helpless, the captives had been broken into their bondage and trained in erotic arts. Now, having served their purpose there, they were to be sold to make way for new blood. Conditioned by training and strictly disciplined, these prime white slaves stoically accepted the attentions of buyers who wandered about the platforms.

Sebastian, his body sleek and oiled, obediently flexed his muscles as a discriminating man patted his bulging triceps. On another platform, Gunther was kneeling while a painted old crone hefted his large balls in her talon-like hand.

Elsewhere, a stunning blonde girl smiled seductively as she spread her legs to facilitate examination by a smartly dressed, swarthy man. It was generally known that he was a buyer for a particularly powerful and wealthy patron whose girls enjoyed a comfortable, pampered life.

A tall suave man watched her quietly from a distance. He discreetly withdrew the small photograph from his pocket: the woman had changed dramatically but it was undoubtedly the one he sought. He saw her gasp as the fellow plucked at her nipples, teasing them into hard button-like protrusion. When the dark-skinned man had finished his inspection and moved on to another platform, Preston strolled over to where the young blonde woman stood displaying her starkly naked body.

Sally Clark was flushed and breathed heavily following the searching, intimate examination by the Arab man but, seeing another's interest, she immediately posed attractively, casting an anxious eye towards the valet who stood nearby.

The newcomer placed his hands upon her hips and gazed up at Sally's face. She looked away, anxious not stare into his eyes. The man asked quietly: "Is your name Sally Clark?"

It was a startling moment. Sally hesitated and gazed wildly about her before whispering! "Yes, Sir."

"Turn around," he ordered. "Bend."

She did as he ordered. After so long as a slave on that island, it was second nature. Modesty was not allowed and Sally had almost forgotten the luxury of it. The guest proceeded to thoroughly examine her naked charms, just like any other buyer, turning her this way and that.

"How were you captured?" he asked, his forefinger gently tracing the outline of the black numbers drawn on her right breast.

"I was jogging in the park near my home. It was a long time ago."

The man nodded and wandered away. What could he want with her, Sally wondered fearfully? How did he know her name? There was no time to consider these questions because already yet another buyer was handling her breasts and passing a hand between her legs. She smiled and spread her legs and thrust out her chest to ease his inspection.

Preston paused by another platform, watching its nude occupant steel herself under the probing attentions of a bizarrely painted old crone who, it was said, ran a string of brothels in the Middle East. Elsewhere, guests wandered about the platforms, occasionally pausing to speak to one of the women.

Unlike Preston, most of the buyers were frequent visitors to the island. Many had already known more than a passing acquaintance with the women on display. These specimens had not been controlled by enforced drug-addiction; they were known quantities and, most importantly, their health was guaranteed. Without the island, the scourge of AIDS would have severely curtailed the guests' promiscuous activities. However, many of these wealthy libertines still maintained their own stables of compliant bond servants.

Other guests were dealers, assessing each item as a speculative purchase for potential resale and profit. Some, like the swarthy man who had now transferred his attentions to a statuesque black girl, were specialist buyers acting on behalf of rich clients who, despite the organisation's impeccable discretion, preferred to remain anonymous. And then there were the pimps and madams, proprietors of vice rings.

Preston watched as the old crone began to claw at Sally Clark, forcing the girl to contort her body this way and that. The organisation did not particularly care what subsequently happened to its wares.

Carlos Fernandez, ever eager to find compliant young women for his estate in Spain, eyed a particularly beautiful Brazilian girl. She had tawny skin, almost olive, and a shiny mane of long black hair. The woman was, in fact, very similar to Serita, his wife. The prominent mound at the junction of her thighs was covered in neatly clipped, silky black hair. Carlos reached out to heft her pert little breasts, fingering the almost coal-black aureolae and nipples. "Turn around. Relax. More."

The woman flinched and inhaled sharply when he tested her rear orifice.

He made a note of the lot number neatly drawn upon her breast.

"Ah, Senor Fernandez. You are in the market again?"

"Always," the courtly Spaniard told the Host, wiping his hand on a silk handkerchief. "Oh, yes, and I am most grateful for your cooperation in respect of Serita."

"It has been my pleasure," the Host replied with a smile. "She is by no means fully tamed. I suspect that your wife is merely feigning compliance until her release."

"If I know the artful Serita that is probably so."

"Then I hope you will not be disappointed."

Fernandez laughed. "I have no fears."

The Host narrowed his eyes somewhat when he saw Preston strolling around Big Hall, pausing to appraise and, occasionally, to examine a displayed beauty. Could it be that this was a potential buyer? The Host swiftly considered the implications, searching for dangers and threats. He could find none. And it was hardly surprising, he concluded, knowing Preston's dominant sexual proclivities. The Host admired this man. Let him buy! His money was as good as that of anyone else. Excusing himself from Fernandez, he wandered over to where John Preston stood.

"Come, Mr Preston, it is time to reunite you with your wife," he said genially. "She will be most surprised to see you."

Preston merely nodded. He followed the Host from Big Hall and up a flight of stairs. They proceeded to a luxuriously appointed apartment where Jade sat apprehensively upon a white leather chair. She was clothed in a demure blue dress. She looked up sharply as the Host entered and hastily rose to her feet. He did not make any comment but merely smiled and then stepped aside to reveal his guest.

Jade's jaw dropped.

"John?"

Preston smiled grimly and held out his hands. "It's over. I've come to take you home."

"No! You can't -"

"It's alright, my dear," the Host said paternally. "You are free to leave. It is all arranged."

"But you don't understand. I don't want to go back. I love my life now."

For once John Preston was fazed. "Love this life?" he asked incredulously. "How can you love being a slave?"

Jade unbuttoned her dress and as the garment fell open she shrugged it off to reveal her practically naked body. Wearing only a garter belt and stockings, Jade clasped her hands behind her neck, proudly displaying magnificent breasts and pierced nipples.

"Don't you see, John? These people have freed me from all my inhibitions. I could never come back now."

"You must," the Host said.

"I am no longer the woman you married, John."

"You will go with your husband."

"No," said Preston, equally firmly. "If she chooses slavery then to hell with her."

He angrily turned on his heals and left the apartment without a backward glance. The Host looked quizzically at Jade, shrugged and hurried after Preston. "What's to be done?" he asked, catching up with his guest.

"Do what you will with her," Preston replied grimly.

"Then she will be stood at auction in Big Hall."

CHAPTER SEVENTEEN

The auction was in full progress and girls waited backstage, silent, withdrawn, and lost in thought, resigned to their fate.

"Next," called the Head Valet.

Angelique, the proud statuesque black woman, naked to the waist and adorned in a great weight of golden necklaces, stepped forward. Clad in a variety of exotic costumes, those who waited their turn on the block could clearly hear the auctioneer as he put each woman through her paces. The bidding was brisk. They heard the auctioneer's smooth tones as he exhorted bidders. It might have been an auction at Southerbys or Christies.

Presently Angelique hurried gratefully from the stage, her now completely naked body covered with a sheen of sweat, heavy breasts rising with panted breath. As each girl returned, sold, naked, perspiring and sometimes weeping, another was thrust through the curtains.

"You," a valet said, propelling a woman into the glare of harsh limelight. Her nipples were pierced and golden rings dangled there.

John Preston almost rose to his feet with a start.

"This is Leila. Armenian, 22 years old."

John Preston eased back, smoking a small cigar and sipping fine Napoleon brandy. He had until that moment calmly watched the pageant of beauty unfold before him, for all the world as if it were an everyday occurrence in his life. The slaves who revealed their charms on stage were indeed beautiful. The whole presentation was calculated to excite interest among eager buyers. He had remained cool and detached. Now, though, as the pierced and bangled beauty stepped forward, Preston's lips tightened.

Leila, expertly directed by the auctioneer, gradually removed the wisps of silk that adorned her body. Naked, she walked the boards of the stage, seemingly oblivious to the bids of those who would buy her. She posed artfully, even mischievously, toying with the bangles at her nipples. Preston swallowed hard. He did not make a bid. Eventually, the auctioneer sold Leila to an Oriental woman whose wide smile revealed several gold teeth.

The lots came, were sold, and quickly left the stage. It was a slickly organised auction. A lovely Asian woman with long black, silky hair, gracefully removed a diaphanous sari. When naked, she performed the stylised dance of a temple girl, legs widely akimbo and hands high, her head traversing on a swanlike neck, and her delightfully firm breasts swaying with a steady rhythm, ensuring a high price.

Male slaves were no less compliant, and no less sought after. Gunther, his cock teased into fierce tumescence, arrogantly strode the stage as male and female voices called their bids. It was a charade, of course, for the German was as submissive as the other slaves; he was ultimately knocked down to the small Arab who had frequently used him.

As for Sebastian, he was docile and pretty upon the stage. It was apparent that he revelled in his bondage. Smiling handsomely, he preened and cavorted, obviously proud of his large, thrusting organ encased in a small leather harness. Sebastian was sold to a wealthy middle-aged American woman who smiled with satisfaction at her capture.

Then a beautiful blonde, stripped to the waist, ran prettily onto the stage, her short tripping steps deliciously jiggling magnificent breasts of cream tipped with honey.

"Now we have lot number 27. English, 23 years old."

Preston leaned forward but, otherwise, he watched impassively as the girl skipped around the stage, her arms straight and strained back. She removed her filmy wraparound skirt and, with a practised high kick, placed her right foot on the auctioneer's tall lectern.

Sally Clark could not quite believe it: she was being sold at auction! And cooperating fully! Her entrance on stage had been purposely humiliating, designed to show off the fluidity of her breasts, she supposed. Stark naked now, the skirt discarded, she extended her right leg and stretched to rest it high upon the auctioneer's rostrum. Her smile at the avidly watching guests was, she hoped, winsome enough. Sally had been well schooled for this moment. The auctioneer stroked her leg, running his fingers up the smooth inner flesh of her thigh, brushing her open sex lips. She held the tortuous position as the auctioneer amused the buyers.

When the music commenced, Sally swayed across the stage in a sinuous and balletic dance that had been so exhaustively rehearsed in the training room. The organisation left little to chance and experts had choreographed the performance. She thrilled at her degradation; being exhibited and sold was, she thought, one of her most delicious experiences. That is a measure of the darker previously hidden side that they had awakened in Sally Clark's sexuality.

"On your knees, legs spread widely," ordered the valet. "Lean right back until your head touches the floor."

This was not part of the choreography. The valets often introduced some surprise for spontaneity. Sally did as he ordered, conscious that her wet sex was opened before the watching guests. Several bids followed. Then she was made to stand, facing first left, then centre, and then right, her back arched like a bow, well displaying her beauty for the buyers. Such was the intensity of the heat in her belly, the warm ache in her vagina, that she feared that she might orgasm there and then. How she hoped that the juices of her sex would not be seen beneath the powerful lights.

"Forty thousand then," the auctioneer eventually announced. "Any more?"

Forty? That was a good price for a common girl. Others had only brought thirty. Sally smiled, straining to see who had made the offer. What kind of bondage awaited her? Then she heard a man call: "Fifty!"

"Fifty," John Preston called, knowing it to be the sealing bid. Sally Clark was led from the stage, purchased.

The Host merely raised his eyebrows. Shrugging, he returned his attention to the auction.

As Sally, nude and perspiring, was led backstage, she heard a commotion and turned to see Serita Fernandez, demurely clad in a black classical belled dress of a Spanish lady.

"No!" stormed Serita, stamping her small feet in anger.

Zorba raised his cane threateningly, but he clearly had no wish to use it; the organisation preferred to display unmarked wares. Serita had allowed the valets to prepare her, thinking that she was about to return to her husband. Now, however, in the anteroom behind the stage, she was in a rebellious mood and steadfastly refused to don the mantilla which a valet held. "I am to be returned to my husband, you dolt," she raged. "The Host will tell you this."

"What is the problem here?" Fernandez asked, entering the anteroom.

"She refuses," the valet replied simply, gesturing towards Serita.

"My dear Serita, you will look charming. The perfect Spanish lady."

"It is a parody," she stormed, snatching the mantilla and hurling it across the room. "I will not play this game for you!"

"Strip the bitch," Fernandez ordered.

The valet grinned hugely and performed his work with relish. He simply tore away Serita's black bodice and her widely-belled skirt. The fastenings had been designed for swift disassembly. Furious, the proud Spanish woman stood naked before her husband.

"Now you see what the animals have done to me," she protested. Her nipples had been painted to match the bright red of her lips and the neat slit of her shaven womanhood was similarly coloured. Half turning, Serita displayed a swatch of black hair, fashioned into the dressed tail of a horse, rising from between the cheeks of her pert little bottom.

"It is the greatest insult. I demand that the disgusting plug be removed along with this ridiculous attachment!"

Fernandez nodded to the attendant, who took great pleasure in sharply applying a strap to Serita's bared buttocks. She shook her hips in pain, causing the tail to swish wildly. "I anticipated this," the Spanish Don said. "Put her into the Host's blindfold mask."

"What clothing will she wear?"

"None. Let the bitch be sold as she is."

Serita gasped in astonished horror. Sold? Her husband would not dare to sell her! But they soon pinioned the struggling Spanish woman and buckled the elaborate opaque mask tightly about her head. It was the first time Serita had worn the device and she was shocked by the sensory deprivation. A scream of anguish echoed dully inside her skull. Minutes later, she stepped blindly forward, directed with sharp raps of a valet's cane.

"Serita is Spanish, very well-connected, aged 28. A diminutive five feet one inch - 90 pounds. The mask conceals her face but I am assured that she is beautiful and unblemished."

A whip urged Serita into action on the stage. After a moments hesitation, sightless and unable to hear, she launched into a demanding display. Her tail swished wildly. Carlos Fernandez chuckled with delight as the Head Valet put her through the degrading routine. At last, Serita was allowed to rest, panting furiously.

"Remove her mask," Fernandez called.

The Head Valet unbuckled the feathered head piece and Serita blinked in the glare of the lights, then placed her hands petulantly upon her hips. "Carlos, you are out there somewhere, you pig," she screeched. "You have had your fun, uh? Now end this charade and we go home."

"My dearest Serita," Carlos answered, stepping forward. "You present a charming spectacle." He turned to the auctioneer. "Sell her to the highest bidder."

"Carlos! You son of a bitch -"

Serita's words were cut short by a stinging whip. She screeched in pain and fell to the floor, writhing beneath a hale of blows. Fernandez' laugh could be heard above her screams. She was made to kneel on all fours, her breasts swinging beautifully.

"Ten thousand..."

"Eleven..."

"Eleven and a half..."

Bidding was slow and the auctioneer struggled to arouse interest. The Head Valet gleefully put Serita through a series of floor exercises, making her roll obediently, stretching and turning. Her exhibition did little to change the view of the bidders, however: the involvement of Carlos Fernandez made the buyers nervous and they shied away from potential trouble.

"Standing to Madam Viner then," the auctioneer said, referring to the proprietor of a notorious brothel in Bangkok. "Surely there must be more bids? Going once ... twice... your last chance, ladies and gentlemen. Standing to Madam Viner at a mere eleven and a half thousand. Asking you for the last time..."

Madam Viner's garishly painted lips parted with a hideous smile as the auctioneer rapped his gavel and confirmed the sale. Serita would serve a harsh bondage in this woman's specialist house of vice. She left the stage, weeping pitifully.

Then Jade Preston strode the boards, heavily clad in an erotic version of chain mail: her legs were encased in tightly fitting stockings of fine-woven steel mesh, and her arms were similarly covered. A looser gleaming mesh hung about her body, offering tantalising glimpses of the promise beneath.

"We come to the final offer today, lot Number 29. Not previously made available for viewing. Sold as seen. This is Jade. Twenty-five years old, brunette, hazel eyes. Extensively re-worked body. Excellent training and specially prepared as an exotic."

Accompanied by a valet, Jade paced the stage and the little bell at her loins tinkled merrily. The trainer flipped a catch on the mesh tunic and it immediately fell away, leaving Jade naked except for metallic stockings and arm-sheaths. Bells had also been attached to her nipple rings.

"A superb specimen," intoned the auctioneer. "Intensively trained and very responsive. She has proven an obedient and, dare I say it, an eager pupil during her time on the island."

Jade, on her knees now and arching backwards, blushed as she heard the ripple of laughter at these remarks. Suddenly, she wanted to rise and flee the stage. However, the trainer was relentless in his demands and she obeyed his every sharp command.

"She has been pierced and ringed, at ears and nose -" Jade shook her head, ringing the tiny bells which dangled from her ears "- both nipples, navel, and, ladies and gentlemen, at her clitoris! Note that the clitoris is unusually large, being almost one inch in length when aroused."

"Fifty-five," a woman called.

"Sixty!"

Jade, led by the valet, perambulated around the stage once more.

"Sixty-five thousand."

Jade was made to jump on the spot and the bells attached to her body tinkled attractively. She was appalled by the humiliation of her exhibition but, also, inexplicably excited and aroused; her prominent clitoris attested to the fact and it was beginning to ache for satisfaction as the little bell swung to and fro.

"One hundred thousand, standing to me personally," cried the Host, and the astonished auctioneer faltered.

"Any advance on one hundred thousand? Are you all done? Once. Asking twice... Gone! That concludes our auction today, ladies and gentlemen."

After the auction an angry John Preston immediately returned to the luxurious suite of rooms allotted to him. He was surprised to find Sally Clark chained at the foot of the bed. Still quite naked. No longer adorned even by the enamelled green collar. She knelt, head lowered, her thighs spaced widely apart. Only the swift rise and fall of full, firm breasts betrayed her anxiety. Preston gazed at the girl and did not speak.

As always, the valet on duty, discreet but ever watchful, had observed his return to the apartment. He tapped on the door and entered without awaiting an invitation. "Compliments of the Host, Sir. He asks me to inform you that confirmation of the transfer of funds is expected before morning. In the meantime, you are free to make use of your purchase."

The valet then offered a number of identically-designed, but differently-sized signet rings. Iron, inlaid with gold, bearing the crest of a fourteen-spoked wheel set in an outer circle. Preston tried two before he found one to fit his long, slender, ring finger.

The fellow showed him the similar ring now worn by the kneeling slave. Any woman so marked, he explained, was available for use to initiates who wore such rings. At all times, in the outside world, her body must be instantly accessible; her style of dress must be so designed to merely lift aside in one easy movement and underwear must never obstruct her intimacies.

He, John Preston, had purchased the woman but, when another man presented the sign, he must yield her willingly. Similarly, as a selected patron of the organisation, its chattels, those owned by others, must submit to the discipline of the iron band he himself now wore. Was it understood?

Preston nodded and gestured to dismiss the curiously-clad fellow. Jade! What obscenities would she suffer in her voluntary bondage? He knew that she had already submitted to the utmost degradation and that she had learned to yearn it, even. She would submit willingly, with wanton abandon, and there was nothing he could do about it. Preston tried to put the thoughts from his mind and he turned his attention to the trembling creature who knelt silently at the foot of his bed, awaiting ravishment: Sally Clark, the woman he had sought and bought.

"What am I to do with you?" John Preston mused. "I suppose you don't want to be free either?"

Nonplussed, Sally gave no reply, nor did she even show that she had heard his words. Preston went to the drinks cabinet and poured himself a large, a very large, brandy. As an afterthought, he poured a small jigger of whisky and brought it to where Sally knelt. Not given permission to speak, she merely shook her head.

"For God's sake," Preston exclaimed in exasperation. "Stand up and take the whisky. And bloody look at me."

Immediately, Sally leapt to her feet. "May I speak?" she asked. "Women here are not allowed to look a man in the face. It is a rule. And alcohol is forbidden to us. However, I am yours to do with as you will."

John Preston frowned as he looked at the nude slave. She stood naked with legs spaced, hands behind her neck, breasts thrust forward, her head bowed deferentially. Sally Clark had been thoroughly conditioned, of that there was no doubt.

"I give you permission to drink the whisky. No - I insist that you drink it. And I order you to look into my face."

Bewildered, Sally did his bidding, shyly looking up from beneath fluttering lashes. Taking the proffered glass, she gulped the whisky down with one swallow. The fiery liquor caused her to splutter and spilt whisky ran down her breasts. She wiped her lips with the back of her hand, suddenly coughing and laughing simultaneously. Preston laughed too, and he steadied her with his arm about her shoulders. Then, suddenly, he found the woman kissing him and, having taken the initiative, she artfully ensnared him, using all the skills so patiently taught in the training rooms.

Sally poured herself against this man who had bought her, grinding her hips against his loins. His member was becoming hard and she could feel it thrusting against her. He hesitated momentarily and, for a second, Sally thought that he was going to throw her off. She would not be denied now! Quickly, the naked woman knelt at his feet, unfastening clothing, rummaging her head eagerly against his thighs, scarcely able to wait until his growing sex was revealed.

Sally won, of course. Resistance completely overwhelmed, John Preston gave in to his own male urges, as all men do. There would be time enough later for any feelings of guilt.

Afterwards, Sally sipped whisky as she idly toyed with one of the manacles that was affixed to the bed head, matter-of-factly telling John Preston of the many times she had served, chained and helpless, in rooms such as this. She smiled when Preston expressed horror and confirmed that his wife would have similarly served on many, many occasions. How could she say anything other?

"Why have you purchased me?"

"A man in London commissioned me to buy you."

"Then who is to be my new owner?" Sally asked anxiously.

Preston could not tell her, for it suddenly occurred to him that he did not even know the Policeman's name. He was saved an explanation when the valet reappeared.

"The Host would like to see you in his quarters, Sir. He wishes to conclude business concerning your wife."

When the man had left, Preston rose to his feet and dressed. "My wife! I wonder what will happen to Jade now?" he said, half to himself.

Sally Clark shrugged. "She will probably serve in the Host's mask. That is how he prefers to use his women."

CHAPTER EIGHTEEN

The feathered mask's leather lining was clammy. Although this ornate and ingenious headgear precluded sight and hearing, Jade could smell its leather, oiled by the perspiration of many women who had worn it before her. She, of course, had also contributed her own sweat. This was nothing new to her. Yet always, she was surprised by the way the mask affected her body: once fitted and tightly buckled, the stillness and blackness seemed to heighten all other bodily sensations.

Her skin became alive even to the most gentle breeze whenever a door opened, or when someone passed close by. The textures beneath her feet, be it of cool smooth marble or of roughly-woven rugs, were suddenly of great significance. When laid down, her flesh pressed and stretched upon a surface, then she found herself identifying it, matching it with patterns, naps and grains in her mind. It was not quite like seeing. And, when the Host touched her intimately, although it was so greatly anticipated, the suddenness always took her by surprise and sent tiny electric shocks through her body.

It was a mental thing, too. Somehow, both dread and delicious anticipation were heightened. She stood, displayed, in the centre of the Host's office, waiting.

"There is some unfinished business between us, Preston. Your wife, Jade." The Host paused to indicate the masked nude. "Your accepting this payment means that you waive all future rights to her. You understand that?"

Preston glanced at the cheque and noted the figure: £100,000.

"And Sally Clark? The girl I purchased?"

The Host shrugged, saying, "You have paid for her. Fifty thousand, I believe. I think that concludes our business. Now, if you will excuse me, I have other matters to occupy me."

When Preston had left, the Host turned to the masked nude and began to unbuckle her outlandish headgear. She smiled, blinked in the light and wiped perspiration from her brow.

"Little Jade," the Host whispered.

Jade did not reply. Her mind was still in turmoil. The Host himself had purchased her! She could not quite come to terms with the fact. Why would he do such a thing? He could, after all, freely take any of the helpless crea-

141

tures who were brought to the island. Why would he want to pay for her?

"I will commission the manufacture of another mask," he said suddenly. "Distinctive and wonderful. You alone shall wear it, my dear. Everyone who sees it will know that you are the Host's personal woman. Will that please you?"

"Of course, Master."

"And tattoos. I shall have you marked with tattoos. Beautiful, intricate works to compliment and enhance your body piercing. My woman! The only one ever to achieve such an accolade. I took a raw and undeveloped creature and moulded her into perfection. You! Created you, even. God took a rib from Adam and created woman. I shall rename you Eve."

The Host's cackling, insane laughter frightened Jade - frightened her as never before, even on this island. She had served him often. Indeed, in past months the man had made a special point of using her frequently, in preference to other women, often encasing her head in his special mask. She had served him abjectly, blind and deaf, surrendering to his inventive lust. There had been fear in that surely enough. But the Host had never appeared like this, not completely mad. His habitual chilling courtesy was gone.

"Eve!" he called.

"Yes, Master?"

"You shall henceforth address me as Zeus, King of all lesser gods!"

He suddenly rushed to rummage in the drawers of his dressing table and, after a frantic search, produced a long, gleaming knife. "We shall make a sacrifice. A sacrifice to me, Almighty Zeus! Let me hear you address me so."

"Zeus!" Jade said, her trembling breasts eliciting tiny tinkling sounds from the bells attached to her nipples. "My master, the Almighty God."

His face was illuminated with delight. He repeated his chosen name again and again, all the time stroking the dagger's lethal blade. Jade kept her distance carefully, moving with feigned nonchalance, smiling, but dreadfully afraid. "My Master, the god of gods," she repeated.

"I must have due homage! Preston denied me my pleasure - I, the mighty Zeus. I created you, didn't I?"

"Yes, my Lord."

"This puny fellow Tranter would have had me killed, you know. Your husband saved me. Oh yes. I planned my revenge... seized Tranter's wife and utterly debauched her. But then" - his brow suddenly creased with concern - "isn't that just what I did to you?"

The Host suddenly wheeled around and placed the tip of his knife at Jade's breast. "And your husband said I was crazy. He even purchased another woman at the auction. Such ingratitude after all my planning."

Jade swallowed hard and, mustered her courage. "He has his own pain, my Lord. Please give me the knife."

The Host seemed nonplussed and the blade quivered, scratching Jade's skin, causing blood to trickle over her soft, yielding breast. She flinched at the slight pain but otherwise maintained a statue-like pose, the rings piercing her breasts rising and falling evenly.

"I am Eve, your hand maiden," Jade blurted with sudden inspiration. "Blood must not soil the hands of the mighty Zeus. Give me the knife, my Lord."

He smiled demonically and lunged towards her, thrusting the knife at her belly. The tip of the blade struck the ring at her navel. It startled her, and the bells at her ears, nipples and clitoris tinkled incongruously as she leapt back.

The Host laughed.

"Let me serve," she stammered, desperately backing away as the deranged man stalked her. "I wish to please you."

There is some doubt as to what happened next. One version of events went like this:

Suddenly the door opened and Jade, thrust aside, screamed. Carlos Fernandez strode forward, followed by two men in business suits. Six valets, clad in their curious costumes, also filed into the spacious suite. The Host was outraged. He brandished the knife, crying, "You dare to intrude!"

Fernandez drew a pistol and simply shot the knife-wielding man. The Host crumpled to the floor, eyes wide in astonishment and Jade screamed and retched as blood trickled from his lips.

"Quite mad," Fernandez said, nudging the Host's lifeless body with his elegantly-shod foot. Then, pointing to Jade, he said: "I shall assume the Host's rights over the pierced beauty. She shall be taken to my estate in Andalusia. The other Russian woman will be disposed of at special auction tomorrow before our guests leave. Kill Tranter and Preston immediately."

Some of the valets cast nervous glances at each other, but none spoke.

Another version of the story, and it is difficult to establish the facts, has it thus:

Jade calmly approached the Host, although her heart beat wildly in fear. She knelt before him, bowed her head deeply and kissed his feet. "I wish to please you," she repeated.

The Host stared down for some moments at the supplicant beauty whose hair fanned around his feet. Holding the knife uncertainly aloft, he gazed at the bow of her back and the valley between her hunched shoulders. Even then, with the fleeting sanity of the mad, he in truth knew himself to be unhinged. Perhaps the quest for revenge against Tranter and his perverse scheme to 'reward' John Preston had completely unbalanced him? Slowly, deliberately, he relaxed his grip upon the knife handle, allowing the weapon to tip from his palm and fall to the marble floor with a metallic clatter.

The Host was weeping when he stooped to grasp Jade. He clasped her tightly. She held him to her soft, pierced breasts, patting his head and crooning like a mother who soothes a hurt child.

"I have Tranter's money," he said. "Now I shall have him killed as he would have killed me. And your husband must die, too. I see now that he is a security risk now that you have spurned him."

Jade stifled a gasp of horror. The Host's madness had not been temporary. Absolute power had, indeed, corrupted him absolutely, like a latter-day Caesar. There was nothing to be done now, however. He summoned valets to his room and issued the order: kill Tranter and Preston.

Then the Host turned to Jade. "You are my special pet, my dear. We shall sell the Tranter woman at special auction tomorrow, before the guests leave. Now, I must speak with Senor Fernandez."

Which of these versions is true? In affairs of intrigue and power, it is often difficult to establish the facts. Even with the clarity of hindsight, truth is often a matter of contention. Perhaps for the purposes here it is unimportant: no matter at whose behest - either that of the Host or Carlos Fernandez, or perhaps both - valets departed on their grim mission, intent on murder.

Two valets entered Tranter's apartment as the American sported with an incredibly innovative Oriental beauty. He died quickly and quietly. Garrotted.

"Get rid of the body," the assassin said, retrieving the thin wire that had bitten so deeply into Tranter's neck.

Meanwhile, in his apartment, John Preston groaned throatily. His whole body stiffened in a muscular spasm and then he suddenly went limp, the victim of an expert, with never a real chance to resist.

"Wonderful!"

Sally knelt up, wiping her mouth and smiling triumphantly. For long, languorous, teasing minutes, her lips, tongue and throat had transported Preston to the very brink of climax, never quite allowing the dam to breach, controlling him, raising and lowering the tempo as she wished. She had learned that, although enslaved, when it came to erotic pleasures it was she who could be the ruler. Ultimately, when she deemed it, she brought him to orgasm.

Preston closed his eyes in mists of pleasure and Sally stretched to kiss his lips, deliberately trailing the tips of her magnificent breasts over his chest.

The mood was broken by an intruder, entering the room unannounced and uninvited. Sally looked up to see Zorba, the valet. She expressed neither surprise nor embarrassment for, like all of the valets, he had often seen her carousing nakedly with guests.

"Mr Preston," Zorba said grimly, clutching a wire garotte. "I have come for you. There is little time. Terrible things are happening."

John Preston squinted through heavy lids. "What sort of terrible things?"

"They say the Host is dead, murdered. Others say not. Maybe Fernandez has taken over - people talk of a coup. It is all uncertain. Tranter is gone, killed - I know that to be true. And now they come for you. It is not safe for you here."

The valet pulled Preston to his feet. He stooped to collect discarded clothing from the floor and thrust the bundle into the naked man's midriff, urging him to leave and dress elsewhere. Convinced, Preston dashed from the room, pausing only to grasp Sally by the wrist. In the moonlit grounds three burly valets were approaching, the sound of their iron-rimmed heels muffled upon grass. Zorba pushed the naked fugitives into a nearby shrubbery.

"You are the duty valet here? We are seeking John Preston."

"He has been transferred to Number 17."

The men muttered oaths of exasperation and hurried off in the opposite direction. Preston immediately emerged from the bushes. There was no doubting the Greek valet now. Without any demur, he and Sally followed Zorba as he led them away from the complex. They did not pause for breath until they had scrambled halfway up the moonlit mountain side. Preston pulled on the trousers. There was no clothing for Sally.

"Perhaps you would now tell me what is happening," Preston demanded, peering from behind a rocky outcrop in search of pursuers.

"Controlling the captives, that is one thing - they often share the strange pleasure and are chosen for it - but killing is not for me. Come, we must move on."

Zorba rose to his feet and began to climb upwards. Preston and Sally followed. Onwards they went, for almost an hour, over rough ground without tracks, climbing high before descending a steep, rocky gorge. Presently, the trio arrived at a small, whitewashed house huddled at the foot of an inland cliff.

"My home," Zorba said simply.

It was a poor, run-down house. The veranda was clothed by a carefully-tended vine and a young boy slept soundly on a rough palliasse there. A scrawny chained dog growled as they approached but it whimpered upon recognising Zorba. The Greek carelessly cuffed the dog away and knelt beside the sleeping boy, gently nudging him.

"Andreas. Wake up, Andreas," he said softly. "I tell you so many times not to sleep outside."

The boy stirred as Zorba carried him into the small house. Preston and Sally followed, watching as he carefully lowered the child onto an unmade bed.

"Your son?" asked Preston.

"My brother. He must often stay here alone. He sleeps outside on warm nights despite my instructions. I should beat him but I cannot."

Zorba caught Sally's ironic smile before averting his eyes; he had often whipped and, sometimes, cruelly marked her with a riding crop.

"Do they know of this house?" Preston asked.

"Yes. But if I return and carry on my duties there is no reason for them to suspect that you are here. I will rest and then go back before they miss me. There is a final auction today... they sell Tranter's woman, Natasha."

CHAPTER NINETEEN

"Natasha. Step forward," the Head Valet called, sharply slapping her rump as he thrust her through the stage curtains. The Russian immediately broke into an elegant prancing trot, hands on the top of her head. Natasha's breasts, protruding through the holes in her red leotard, bounced rhythmically as she circled the stage.

"The special sale today: Natasha, 26 years of age, standing five feet six inches and weighing 110 lbs. See how she moves. Wonderfully lithe and supple - hardly surprising since she was formerly an international gymnast, ladies and gentlemen. Imagine this one in your bed, a genuine bisexual, very experienced and utterly subservient."

Natasha flashed her eyes at the auctioneer but continued to prance around the stage. Then, on a given signal, she cart-wheeled spectacularly, coming to a perfect, motionless halt beside the podium. The audience cheered and clapped. Without awaiting instruction, Natasha peeled off her leotard. Music commenced and the nude woman launched into an energetic and elegant gymnastic floor routine.

"Thirty," a woman's voice called, and Natasha blanched.

"Thirty-five..."

"Forty..."

The object of their bidding stood rigidly to attention as the auctioneer began to describe her physical attributes. She meekly allowed him to point to each feature with his cane, obediently sucking in her stomach and thrusting her breasts forward.

"Come now," the auctioneer chided as the bids crept up. "This is a special acquisition who has been intensively trained. No effort has been spared. Do I hear fifty thousand?"

"Fifty..."

"Any advance?"

Natasha held her breath as the auctioneer surveyed the room with hawk eyes.

"Going once, then, twice... Sold to Mr Wafiq!"

Meanwhile, Preston and Sally Clark had arrived at a tiny sea cove on the south side of the island. Preston dragged Sally along a small shingle beach. He now wore the curious uniform of a valet - one he had found in Zorba's hut - hoping that it might offer some protection if they were sighted. Sally

147

was nude, at her own insistence, for she reasoned that few on the island would think anything unusual in a valet escorting a naked slave.

Shading his eyes from the sun, Preston looked out to sea. A floating platform was moored a hundred yards or so away from the shore and a rowing boat slowly edged towards it. In contrast, a swift launch cleaved the surf, returning to the quay beyond the promontory. As they watched, a helicopter rose.

"Many guests are leaving today with the women they bought at the auction," Preston observed. "It will probably be a long time before so much transport is available on the island again. Can you swim?"

Kicking off his buckled shoes, and removing the short red jacket and full white shirt, John Preston began to wade into the sea. Sally ran into the gentle surf and, after a few strides, plunged forward to swim with an elegant breast stroke. The pair made slow progress. Preston insisted on taking a wide, indirect course, swimming far to the left, out to sea, before turning to approach the deck from the far side. After almost half an hour in the water, they came within hearing distance of the gently bobbing platform. A valet was talking to the boatman: "How many more?"

"Two. The remainder are leaving from the island."

A luxury yacht slipped past, quietly leaving the bay. Preston was surprised to see a number of similar craft moored there; evidently many guests had arrived in their own boats. The bay had been obscured from view in the tiny cove, and he had not visited the quay since arriving on the island. He cursed silently. Neither Zorba nor the girl had told him of the number of seagoing craft that were present. Approaching them from this point, however, meant risking being seen by the boatman. A helicopter whirred overhead, whipping the water into eddies.

"Come on. Quickly!" Preston yelled, diving beneath the surface and kicking strongly towards the platform.

Inhaling deeply, Sally followed, digging into the last reserves of her ebbing strength. Beneath the surface she could see Preston in the clear water but it was less easy to keep pace with him. Nevertheless, her lungs almost bursting, she managed to swim beneath the platform.

She surfaced beside Preston, under the floating deck, gasping for air in the low space between floating pontoons and the timbers they supported. The platform shuddered as the helicopter landed, causing water to splash wildly and swamp the spluttering fugitives. They clung to a bobbing pontoon, waiting for the turbulence to subside. Then Preston silently slipped under the float. Peeping over the deck, underneath the polished fuselage, he could see a large obese man ushering a young woman towards the cockpit. The pilot, he judged, had remained at his controls. Sally surfaced alongside, clinging to the edge of the timbers.

Hoisting himself athletically aboard the platform, Preston wrenched open the nearside hatch. The pilot looked around in surprise, his jaw turning conveniently to meet a swinging clenched fist. He slumped forward, and Preston tore the communications set from the man's head before thrusting him from the cockpit.

"What the -" the fat guest yelled. "Hey!"

Sally scrambled alongside Preston, who was already settling himself into the pilot's seat. Even as she struggled to fasten the straps about her dripping body, the helicopter began to rise from the floating pad.

"You can fly this thing?" she asked.

Preston manoeuvred the machine expertly, climbing high and swinging away to the west.

The Policeman's opened wide as John Preston ushered Sally into the London office.

"Dad!" Sally cried in astonishment, rushing to hug her father.

John Preston watched in astonishment as they embraced. "You set all this up? My invitation to the Bond-Age, everything?"

Sally stepped forward to squeeze John Preston's hand, smiling wistfully. He looked down at the distinctive iron band upon her ring-finger. He knew that beneath Sally's demure buttoned shirt-dress she was naked, instantly available and accessible to all men who knew the sign. The Policeman, her father, knew nothing of this; he turned away to gaze through the window at the London skyline.

As Preston toyed with the iron ring on Sally's finger, she somehow knew that in his mind at that moment was the terrible realisation that Jade would be forever enslaved by irrepressible, darker desires. Like Sally, Jade loved her enslavement and she would continue to serve, surrendering herself to any stranger who wore the iron ring.

Sally glanced at her father, whose back was turned. She leaned forward to kiss Preston gently on the cheek. "You are still my owner," she whispered softly. "I am your slave until you sell me to another."

John Preston smiled slightly as Sally lowered her gaze.

SILVER MOON TITLES

Barbary Slavemaster
by *Allan Aldiss*

ISBN 1897809018

'It was in 1809 (by the Christian calendar) that the Pasha consulted me regarding the purchase of a woman - something which one would have thought to be a routine matter, and certainly not one in which it was either necessary or desirable to involve a renegade Englishman such as myself. But the next orders were clear ... to train and then march a coffle of white slavegirls into the interior as gifts with which to bribe the cruel tribesmen to abandon their liaison with Napoleon..'

Erica: Property of Rex
by *Rex Saviour*

ISBN 1897809026

Rex is a strict disciplinarian and also a religious bigot. He finds himself in a situation that causes him great concern when a teenager whose behavior he considers sinful comes under his complete control. He vows not to be too severe with her, but she is very provocative, and punishing her arouses strange desires that threaten his self control..

Barbary Slavegirl
by *Allan Aldiss*

ISBN 1897809034

It is 1810 and Rory Fitzgerald, the renegade who serves in the Turkish Jannissaries, is on an official visit to Malta, where he is publicly insulted by a fiery young Irish girl. Thus begins a story set in the days when captured European women really were sold like animals in the markets - the girl is shipwrecked and enslaved, sold in the market, and becomes a brothel slave, then chained to an oar in a galley - which belongs to the man she has insulted!

SILVER MOON TITLES

Biker's Girl
by *Lia Anderssen*

ISBN 1897809042

Set in the near future, this is the story of a beautiful young runaway who glories in sex and exhibitionism, and is an out-an-out masochist. Due to an unfortunate incident she is naked when she meets a group of Bikers and naked she remains through many painful episodes. Then the Biker of her fancies sweeps her off her feet, doubtless to live happily ever after (or rather until Biker's Girl On The Run) as his handmaiden...

Bound For Good (A 3 in 1 Special)
Authors *Gord, Saviour, Darrener*

ISBN 1897809050

Bound For Good, by Gord - To help him write the ultimate bondage novel, Sam recruits the stunning Jannine - who soon finds herself bound up in her role. Surely this IS the ultimate bondage novel!

Robin:Property of Ogoun, by Rex Saviour (author of Erica) - Suppose an exotic young lady jumps into your taxi at 2am on Christmas Eve. She has no money, no possessions, no passport, nowhere to go. Do you return her to the sadistic husband whom she has just robbed and scarred for life? Or do you keep her for yourself?

Teacher's Pets, by Adam Darrener - End of term and Mr. Robinson is having trouble with two over-nubile school leavers - fortunately these young vixens relish the punish they have earned.

The Training of Samantha
by *Lia Anderssen*

ISBN 1897809077

Here comes another Anderssen heroine who loses her clothes in chapter one and never recovers them. Samantha, a very nubile young lady, is accused of drug smuggling in a third world country, and instead of prison accepts a way of life which, brutal and degrading though it is, she relishes not only as a wanton but as a rabid masochist.

SILVER MOON TITLES

Barbary Pasha
by *Allan Aldiss*

ISBN 1897809085

When Jane arrives in Malik her fiancé is away in the
interior. But there is no problem - the Pasha will look after her.
She will be an honored guest of course, not a member of his
harem - or will she? Things soon get out of hand in the company of this tyrant - cruel, dominating, fascinating, here is a
real man, a man one could come to worship...

Circus of Slaves
by *Janey Jones*

ISBN 1897809107

When Holly and her friends set out in search of adven-
ture, joining Mr Columbus's Speciality Circus seems like a good
thing to do. BUT...

The Hunted Aristocrat
by *Lia Anderssen*

ISBN 1897809113

Meet Lady Antonia de Martinique, a beautiful young English aristocrat who finds herself an innocent abroad in a strange land. During a
series of erotic adventures, her innocence is lost, along with her clothes.
In this helpless state she falls into the hands of the mysterious Count, who
imprisons her in his castle. Chained and naked, she submits to his power,
becoming a plaything for his friends and his servants alike. Only her
betrothed, Lord Percy, can rescue her from the cruel regime to which the
Count subjects her. But does this luscious young masochist wish to be
rescued?

SILVER MOON TITLES

Barbary Enslavement
by *Allan Aldiss*

ISBN 189780914X

We are back in the days of the Napoleonic Wars, when the Barbary pirates were free to ravage the Mediterranean Coastlines and Islands, and carry off white women to be sold in the slave markets of Tunis, Algiers and our fictional port of Marsa, whose Pasha has ordered Rory Fitzgerald to capture a certain Italian Contessa as a gift for the Sultan.

Rorig's Dawn
by *Ray Ameson*

ISBN 1897809166

Enter the world of Khaea; another world, an alternate Earth perhaps, but one where swords and sorcery clash, with the rewards of riches and power, and sumptuous sweet-bodied slavegirls!

Biker's Girl On The Run
by *Lia Anderssen*

ISBN 1897809174

Lia Anderssen has single-handedly established a new genre of erotic story - one in which the heroine is totally naked throughout, and gets punished for it. So when a rival gang captures Lia (who we met in Biker's Girl) it is only to be expected that she is naked at the time!

SILVER MOON TITLES

Caravan of Slaves
by *Janey Jones*

ISBN 1897809204

Jo has lost her job - Daisy is broke - Cassie has been jilted. Then, one Monday morning in May, each girl's path is crossed by a gipsy...

Slave to the System
by *Rosetta Stone*

ISBN 1897809239

It wasn't Julia who was smuggling – it was her boyfriend. But when hard drugs were discovered in HER luggage, HE was conveniently – for him! – absent.

The penalty was death – or several years servitude.

So Julia accepted servitude, which turned out to involve humiliation, beatings and abuse.

Being a slave to the system turned out badly – or did it? Seemingly there was a certain something about servitude that appealed to a secret lust at the heart of her....

Barbary Revenge
by *Allan Aldiss*

ISBN 1897809255

Amanda Aston makes a grave mistake when she ridicules certain rich and powerful men from Arabia on television- she ends up in the hands of a modern slave dealer, and when it comes to revenge she soon encounters old cruelties not far beneath the surface of modern life...

SILVER MOON TITLES

The Drivers
by *Henry Morgan*

ISBN 189709263

New Author due February '96

SILVER MINK TITLES

When The Master Speaks
by *Josephine Scott*

ISBN 1897809093

In 1869 Clarisse runs away from her country home, and excessive parental discipline, to the delights of London, where she finds discipline can have a deeper and more pleasurable meaning than she ever realized. In 1969 Lauren leaves the country - and a broken relationship - for those same delights, where she also finds that love can have painful yet pleasurable overtones. In a house in Fleet Street past and present blend... a fascinating tapestry of pain and pleasure.

Amelia *(A Tale of Punishment and Retribution)*
by *Josephine Oliver*

ISBN 1897809131

Amelia falls under the sway of a 'Country Gentleman' whose attitude towards women was learned among the slave owners of an American Plantation of the 1850s. He submits her to deeper and deeper discipline and degradation, until at last the tables are turned ... and, as Mistress, Amelia knows exactly how to exercise her new won powers.

The Darker Side
by *Larry Stern*

ISBN 1897809158

What Wendy did, above all, was open my mind to the idea, and the acceptance of that notion, that love has a darker side, that there can be intense sensual pleasure in acts of humiliation and chastisement, that the stroke of the whip can stimulate as effectively as a kiss or a caress. So the stories that form this volume are drawn from that darker side...

SILVER MINK TITLES

The Training of Annie Corran
by *Terry Smith*

ISBN 1897809190

Stig is a pimp, a larger-than-life figure who has many ways of training his women - including 'Mr Sting', an innocent looking length of bamboo which can turn any woman's body to quivering jelly.

Sonia
by *RD Hall*

ISBN 1897809212

The strap she relished: easy to tell. "It covers me as well as wakes me ... it is comforting, warm - you work it well - it is fire on a dark night."

The cane she was still uncertain about. "You teach me if it means business I think?" "Yes my little one, yes."

The whip was small, it was for youngsters, yet it gave me the horror. "Will, you are not trying! Listen, I will tell you some things from my school days: after you will not shrink from giving me whippings..."

The Captive
Author *Amber Jameson*

ISBN 1897809220

Zacora is an amazingly beautiful young lady, where a woman's only duty is to obey and pleasure her man.
Betrayed and shamed, when is sent to another land to be auctioned. Here it is the women who dominate, and the men into whose hands she falls take their bitter revenge upon her. But even in the midst of the worst beatings and humiliation Zacora is bound by her upbringing to please.
The man she pleases most is the Pretender to the throne— can her sweet nature affect the behavior of a Kingdom?

SILVER MINK TITLES

Dear Master
Author *Terry Smith*

ISBN 1897809247

Reading a naughty book reveals the truth about herself to Susan Dixon. She needs a Master! Someone to discipline her, mould her, beat her if she is disobedient, change her from the cute and provocative but very child–like young woman that she is into the alluring sophisticated person she longs to become.

The author sounds like a true Master, a man she can love, a man she can write to: *'Dear Master, Please let me serve you...'* But what of the recipient of this sweet trusting letter? Is he worthy of her or will he take advantage of her innocence, make of her an erotic toy to be used and abused and shared with his friends?

Sisters in Servitude
by *Nicole Dere*

ISBN 189780928X

When Fran set out to visit her sister on a remote Island she did not expect to be met by her sister's boyfriend—with a pair of handcuffs!

And then to discover that they were both to be trained to the tastes of the sadistic Prince Salman....

Things were to get worse, far worse, before they got better!

Cradle of Fear by *Krys Antarakis*
January 1996

Owning Sarah by *Nicole Dere*
March 1996
(see picture)

Silver Moon   Silver Mink